# Books by Alina

The Frost Brothers
- Eating Her Christmas Cookies
- Tasting Her Christmas Cookies
- Frosting Her Christmas Cookies
- Licking Her Christmas Cookies
- Resting Grinch Face

The Wynter Brothers
- Good Elf Gone Wrong
- Elf Against the Wall

The Richmond Brothers
- The Art of Awkward Affection
- The Art of Marrying Your Enemy

Christmas in Harrogate
- Sleigh Bells & Slaughter
- Holly & Homicide
- Crime & Candycanes

Check my website for the latest news:
http://alinajacobs.com/books.html

# Peppermint AND Poison

A Holiday Cozy Romantic Mystery

# Peppermint and Poison

ALINA JACOBS

*Summary: When a flaming corpse falls out of the town Christmas tree and straight through my roof, my holidays officially go up in smoke. Suddenly my unhinged ex–best friend is telling everyone I murdered her therapist/secret lover, and she's even hired a trench-coat-wearing private eye who insists I'm hiding something. All I want is to keep my struggling café afloat—not chase down killers or get distracted by the grumpy detective who thinks I'm guilty. But as more bodies start dropping, I'm forced to play sleuth to save my business, my reputation, and what's left of my holiday spirit...before Christmas turns deadly for all of us.*

*For everyone who's successfully*
*restrained themselves from*
*murdering a relative...*

*No, no, no, now that's all wrong*
*This thing will never make a present*
*It's been dead for much too long*
*Try something fresher, something pleasant*

*–Making Christmas*

# CHAPTER 1

# Willow

"I want an actual Yule log this year."

"Gran, no. No one wants to burn down the Christmas market."

"I pay taxes. I should get a bonfire," she rails as I shoo her out of the Jingle Bites stall. "Let's see the Grinch burned in effigy."

"Excuse me!" A woman stomps up to me. "Excuse me! I want a refund on this Christmas crackle candy." She waves a half-eaten bag of chocolate at me. "It made Brayden sick!" She points at a green-looking five-year-old.

I try to look sympathetic and not annoyed. "Ma'am, I can't give you a refund. Most of the bag is gone."

"This is an outrage. I want to speak to your manager!"

"I own the Jingle Bites Café and the associated Christmas market stall," I tell her. "I am the manager."

"Then I want to speak to the mayor."

"I think she's busy with the tree-lighting ceremony that's about to happen." I gesture to the humongous evergreen. Gideon Cross is putting the finishing touches on its lights.

Then I see her. No, not the mayor.

*Her.* Taylor Grace Nicole Glass, my ex-friend and toxic coworker, is powering through the crowd, sending children screaming and reindeer howling.

Not really, but I want to run and hide, and I would if I didn't have an irate Karen in my face, trying to get free candy out of me.

"You've been sending me to voicemail!" Taylor Grace shrieks.

All the people at the Christmas market—most of whom are drunk on alcohol, Christmas treats, or both—turn and stare as Taylor Grace descends into an angry tirade.

I'm cursing the fact that I inherited such a good stall placement because this close to the mega Christmas tree? I'm the star of the Christmas pageant.

"Um, hey, what's up, Taylor…?"

She's flanked by two men: one in tweed with elbow patches and wire frames, the other taller, handsome, broad shouldered. He would be cute if he weren't wearing a trench coat and a literal fedora.

*Freak.*

"*Uhhhh…*" Her eyes bug out as she mocks me. "Uh, what's up? *What's up?* You mean aside from the fact that you cut me out of my own bakery that I helped start?"

"Oh, is it time for our weekly scheduled freak-out?"

"You see—" Taylor turns to Dr. Jonah Merriweather, therapist and elbow-patch wearer. Hack, more likely, if he can't see through her lies. "This is what I'm saying. She is emotionally abusive."

"Now, Willow," Jonah says in a condescending tone, "Taylor just wants to tell you her truth."

"I really don't have time to get into a three-hour circular argument with you right now." I glare at Taylor Grace.

"Taylor Grace set a boundary," Dr. Merriweather says in an annoying, nasally voice. "And you need to respect that boundary and listen to what she is trying to say. Really *hear* her. I need you to practice *active listening*, Willow."

"That's not how boundaries work..." I roll my eyes.

"Um, ma'am, I am still waiting on my refund," the customer interjects. "You need to take care of personal business when you're off the clock."

"*Personal business?*" Taylor Grace's shriek reaches a deafening level.

Townspeople swarm in front of my stall, probably hoping for a fight to break out.

"You think this is *personal* business? You've been telling people the Jingle Bites Café is your *personal* business? You would be nothing without me. You're so stupid and lazy and uncreative, you never could have come up with any of these new Christmas treats without me. And instead of giving me full ownership of the bakery like you promised, you're trying to steal it from me!"

"That was never the deal..."

"It should have been." Her face is red with anger. "You did nothing to build this bakery."

"Are you kidding me?" I holler at her, falling for the argument trap. "You would half-ass ideas that I then had to find a way to make work and taste good because you went around town telling people we were going to have maple reindeer doughnuts, even though we don't have a doughnut fryer, so I had to buy it on credit. There are a thousand things like that, and now all of my money is sunk into this godforsaken bakery."

"No, you didn't," she says automatically.

"Yes, I did. I literally have bank statements."

"So now you're accusing me of stealing money?" Her tone immediately changes, and her eyes start watering.

Crocodile tears.

"Willow is calling me a thief, Hughes."

Fedora gives her a sympathetic look.

Idiot.

"This conversation doesn't feel safe," she says, chin wobbling.

"You started this fight." My teeth grind. "You came over here, while I'm trying to sell Christmas candy to keep this business afloat, literally just to start an argument."

"She's gaslighting me!" Taylor Grace turns to Dr. Merriweather. "Do you hear her?"

"Yes," he says soothingly. "Willow has an anxious attachment style."

"No, Willow does not," I snap. "Willow is tired of running this bakery by herself while Taylor Grace gets all the money, does no work, and takes all the credit for it."

"It's my bakery," my ex-best friend sniffles.

"You are emotionally deregulated," Dr. Merriweather declares, looking down his nose at me.

"Um, Taylor Grace might be paying for you to dish out toxic therapy speak, but I'm not," I hiss.

"Taylor Grace is trying to speak her truth, and you need to listen."

"Isn't that what Tall, Dumb, and Handsome is here for?" I nod to Trench Coat.

"What?" The young guy next to them shakes his head. "I'm not—"

"You're wearing a fedora. You really complete this little trio of toxic TikTok culture come alive like Frosty the Snowman."

"Hughes is my private investigator." Taylor Grace flips her hair. "He's collecting evidence that proves you have maliciously and willfully tried to steal my bakery."

"She tried to be nice and work with you," Fedora says, "but obviously, you want to do this the hard way." He cracks his knuckles like this is some Martin Scorsese Netflix special.

"What the fuck? I'm in Crazy Town."

Then Taylor Grace screams like she's being murdered. "Get that little freak!"

Taylor points at Gideon, who is crouching down in my stall.

"I told you, not here," Dr. Merriweather hisses at Gideon Cross.

"I'm not here for either of you." Gideon holds up the end of an extension cord. "Plug this in for the tree." He sticks it at me.

"Can you say please?" I sigh.

"Hollis said I could." He glares.

"Sorry!" Hollis shouts, rushing in, her arms full of boxes.

Taylor Grace's nostrils flare as she stares at Hollis. "Another traitor."

Hollis sighs. "Taylor..."

"It's Taylor Grace," my ex-best friend snaps at Hollis, who runs behind the counter to start taking orders from the people in line. "And you have her working for you now?" My ex-best friend turns on me, furious. "She's replacing me. You pushed me out."

"Yes, Taylor, I told you I needed help. It's the Christmas rush."

"And now you're going to hire him, too, I bet." She points at Gideon, who is glaring at the therapist.

"He's just rigging up the Christmas tree, Taylor. Because not everything is a vast conspiracy to take you down. The rest of us in town are trying to put on a nice Christmas market. Not everything is about you."

"Gaslighting!" Taylor Grace shrieks.

Hollis winces.

"They're all gaslighting!"

"No one is gaslighting you except that therapist," Gideon tells her as he checks the cable. "He's putting all these ideas in your head."

"Don't listen to him, Taylor Grace." Dr. Merriweather puts his arm comfortingly on Taylor Grace's back. "He is, in my professional opinion, mentally ill."

"Is that your new boyfriend?" Gideon nods to Fedora.

"Um—" Fedora frowns.

Taylor Grace giggles.

Dr. Merriweather looks shocked.

"I think we need to have another therapy session about this."

"Beware," Gideon tells Fedora. "You stick your dick in crazy, and look what happens. Run, brother. Don't walk. It's not too late to save yourself."

"Gideon and Willow are working against me!" Taylor Grace screams. "I bet you two are in a relationship behind my back."

"I don't have time to be in a relationship because I'm trying to run the shop and clean up after your mess!" I holler. "Now purchase something or get out of my Christmas stall."

“This isn’t over,” Taylor Grace shrieks at me. “Karma is going to get you.”

“I wish karma would actually help during the Christmas rush if karma’s so concerned about the state of the Jingle Bites Café!” I scream after them.

The Karen clutches her little boy.

I grab a bag of Christmas crunch candy and thrust it at her. “Here. Merry fucking Christmas.”

“Well. We won’t be patronizing this stall anymore. And I’m going to complain to the mayor and the grand master of the Christmas market.” She shoos the little boy away.

Fuck them, I am emotionally deregulated.

I slump against the counter and breathe in the scents of snow and Christmas. Normally, it’s my favorite time of the year. I love the way the entire small town of Harrogate comes out to put on a month of Christmas festivities. I love the Christmas food. I even love Gran’s annual holiday sweater party.

Now?

Christmas is officially ruined, and we’re barely recovered from Thanksgiving. Thanks to Taylor Grace, the Jingle Bites Café is in the red. I’m so stressed I can barely sleep. Unfortunately, all the stress hasn’t caused a loss of appetite, so none of my clothes fit.

Pro tip: An oversized scarf helps hide the fact that you can’t zip up your jacket.

And because Christmas is the time that retailers are supposed to fatten up before the long, cold march to summer, I can’t even dig out of this hole, because Taylor Grace is determined to take not just half but all of the company.

Well, all of nothing is nothing. Taylor Grace thinks she can run the Jingle Bites Café? No way.

I wish I'd never gotten involved with her.

You meet someone you think is a kindred spirit, then they turn the tables on you as soon as you're trapped with them.

"Who was that hot guy?" My friend Josie skips into the stall, diamond ring glittering on her finger.

"I hope you didn't forget your baby at the Gingerbread Pantry again. Did you?" I inspect her baby-less state.

Josie giggles. "That was just once! It's been an adjustment to motherhood." She grimaces. "But he's fine. He is with Mace. But all I do is talk about babies. I want to talk about men. Who was that?"

"The creep in the fedora?"

"And a trench coat! Yum!"

"Some of us have outgrown our middle school crushes on guys with trench coats as their whole personality."

"He liked you! I saw him at the reindeer jerky stall. They really upped their game from last year. I don't feel sick at all after eating there."

Josie eyes the peppermint bark. Her gaze keeps flicking to it then to me.

"Go on, have some candy." I push the glass jar over to her.

"Candyyyy!" She stuffs it in her face. "So," she says around the mouthful of chocolate, "let's strategize how you're going to ask him out."

"I'm not asking him out. I don't want him in my life."

"He likes you! I saw him making googly eyes at the stall."

"Ugh, no he wasn't."

"Do you have ice cream?"

I hand Josie some Yule log swirl and gummy polar bears because I know how my friend likes her ice cream.

"I don't have time for a man anyway."

"No, you need a boyfriend. You said you're decentering Taylor Grace, right?"

"Trying. I keep getting sucked back in."

"A man will help."

"Yeah, well, not Fedora. Taylor Grace is absolutely after him. And it's so obvious he's into her. Men love a psychotic, manic pixie dream girl."

"It's so unfair that someone so awful gets to look like a trophy wife," Josie muses.

"Do you want to go get a turkey sandwich or a salad? Something not candy-coated."

"Yeah, probably should. I had doughnuts for breakfast and a fruitcake parfait for lunch. Protein's good if you're nursing, right? It's nice that you have this stall, though. We can see the Christmas tree from here. I'd say I'm excited for Christmas except Mace wants to take all the kids to Seattle for the holidays."

"That sounds…"

"Like a lot, right?" she says as we wait in line for a Santa's pizza cone.

"One per person!" Lydia announces loudly. "Hey, girls!" She hands us our steaming pizza cones. "Oh, Josie, I think Davy might have Aiden over for a sleepover tonight. Just wanted to let you know. You can drop him off with Travis if you don't want him."

Josie shrugs. "We won't even notice."

Lydia gives me a sympathetic look. "I heard my sister go off on you."

"Yep, right on time."

"She's just gotten worse and worse. She and Damien got in a fight. He claims she's cheating on him. She claims his mother is out to get her." Lydia makes a face. "I had to listen to it for three hours last night. I literally can't take it anymore. Travis wants me to call her therapist."

"Good luck," Josie says, dunking her stuffed-crust cheese stick into the gooey cheese-and-pepperoni dip. "Willow says she and the therapist are…" She mimes rolling her hips.

"Oh, great. She's going to be insufferable when he dumps her."

"Maybe his wife will take her out"—Josie snorts—"and we'll have a wonderful Christmas after all."

They both laugh.

"We shouldn't joke about that, I guess."

"Hey, we've created life, and we can take it away."

"Amen." Lydia pats her pregnant belly.

"Are you going to have gingerbread churros again this year?" Josie asks as we make our way through the excited crowd toward the huge Christmas tree.

It rivals the one at Rockefeller Center, and unlike that tree, this one gets bigger every year because it's planted smack-dab in the center of the town square.

"Yeah, I'll do them Friday." I poke at my Santa's pizza dip. "I'm so sick from the altercation with Taylor Grace, I can't even eat. I don't know if I can survive this Christmas season."

"Yesss! You should use the churros as the opener for Mr. Tall, Dark, and Handsome." She nudges me. "Might brighten up your holiday season. Can't spell 'stress relief' without sex!"

Fedora is across the crowd, a head taller than everyone else, especially with that stupid hat. He even has a little paper in the band, like he's a 1940s private eye or something.

Mayor Loring climbs up onto the makeshift stage to address the crowd. "Merry Christmas, everyone!"

Josie cheers and whoops for her sister-in-law.

I sigh and clap.

"Welcome to another season of the Harrogate Christmas Market, the biggest in the Northeast! As your mayor, I'm going to officially kick us off. Let's light that Christmas tree."

Ida, resident senior, owner of the general store, and one of the Christmas committee members, hands her an oversized decapitated Santa head.

"Now, to figure out who will do the honors, we're going to hold our first raffle of the season." She reaches into the head. "We want to showcase one of our Christmas market stalls." She opens up the paper. "The Christmas tree lighter will be Stall Two-Forty-Four," she announces.

Crap.

"Ooh, that's you! That's the Jingle Bites Café!" Josie whoops loudly and jumps and waves.

Taylor Grace rushes up to the stage, screaming, "That's my café too!"

"Fine, Taylor Grace. You can do it." I sigh and turn to leave.

"Why don't you both push the button together?" Megan offers.

"I don't want to push it anyway," Taylor Grace crosses her arms, nose in the air.

"Whatever." I flip the oversized switch.

Nothing happens.

I flip it back and forth.

Gideon fiddles with the electrical wires leading to the tree.

"It was working this morning… Aha. Try it again."

I flip the switch.

The lights on the tree blaze, and everyone cheers.

Then I smell roasting pork over the sugar-and-spice smell of the Christmas market. The lights get brighter, then several of them pop, sparking.

The fire department gets ready.

"First fire of the season, boys!"

They cheer.

"No one is burning this tree down," Mayor Loring threatens.

Suddenly, all the lights go out. Smoke wafts out of the tree, and the fire department aims its hoses.

"What is that smell?"

"I thought the reindeer barbecue was next Monday," people whisper.

I have a sinking feeling that my bad day is about to get much worse.

The branches of the tree move. There's rustling like a big animal is in there.

People in the audience scream.

Hunter, Meg's husband, jumps up on the stage protectively. Fedora does the same for Taylor Grace.

I have no man who cares about my safety, so I shove the branches out of the way.

More rustling, then branches creak, and a corpse falls out of the tree to swing silently, flames crackling, wrapped merrily in Christmas tree lights. There's a creak and a *snap*, then the corpse falls out of the sky…

Right onto the roof of my stall.

"Water!" The fire department douses the Jingle Bites stall.

"Oh my god!" Taylor Grace's screams pierce the night. "Jonah! Jonah! Someone help him!" She rushes to him.

Fedora holds her back, away from the smoldering corpse.

"Jonah! Oh, poor Jonah!" Then she turns to me, face a mask of fury. "You killed him, Willow Price! You killed Dr. Merriweather!"

# CHAPTER 2

# Hughes

*The snow is falling like powdered sugar over a city that hasn't been sweet in years. Christmas lights blink down crooked alleys, but they can't outshine the shadows. That's where I come in. Name's Hughes. Hughes Whitaker. Private eye. While the rest of the world is stringing tinsel and kissing under mistletoe, I'm chasing down a case colder than a reindeer's nose. And let me tell ya—nothing good ever hides in a stocking that big…*

"Hughes, you talking to yourself again? I swear." My nana swats my arm.

She gets jostled by the townspeople who are eager to catch a glimpse of the crime scene.

"You're a good-looking kid. You need to stop all that PI nonsense and find a nice girl. No woman wants a man who plays dress-up. Early retirement isn't mentally healthy for someone your age."

"I'm not—this is a real private investigation firm. I'm living my childhood dream, Nana." I set down my notepad. "This is my first real case!"

"I thought that gal with the crazy eyes was your first case."

"My damsel in distress."

Nana just raises her eyebrows.

"Now, Hughes, you need a warmer coat. That thin trench coat's not going to cut it. Why don't you wear that puffer jacket I bought you for your birthday?"

"That's not what PIs wear, Nana. And I'm working here. This murder is probably part of the Taylor Grace case. It's all connected."

The damsel herself is draped artfully over the body of her beloved therapist, sobbing. A young pregnant woman—Lydia, I see in my notes—takes Glass, her sister, and leads her away as she screams—wails, really.

"Willow killed him!" Taylor Grace sobs as the paramedics load Dr. Merriweather into a body bag then onto a stretcher.

"You'd think they were married the way, that girl is carrying on," my grandmother mutters.

"Mary Lou! Mary Lou, yoo-hoo!" Nana's elderly neighbor, Beryl, huffs up. "Did you see the body?"

Willow, the woman my damsel in distress has hired me to investigate, is grumpy in her layers of clothes. "Of all the horrible luck. Fuck Christmas."

"At least your stall didn't burn up." Josie pats Willow's arm.

"It's waterlogged!" She glares at me when she sees me staring.

"Oh! I see you two know each other." Nana beams.

"This is Hughes," Beryl tells Willow. "He's just moved back to town. From England."

"You don't sound like you're from England."

"I was just getting some experience. Walking the same streets as Sherlock Holmes."

"You were supposed to come back with some sexual experience." Nana wags her finger at me. "Are you still a virgin?"

"Nana!" I hiss, face hot.

"Not if Taylor Grace has anything to do with it," Willow snorts.

"Isn't this an exciting start to the holiday season? You got here just in time. Didn't he, Willow?" Beryl giggled.

"And here we thought Santa forgot all about us." Nana claps a hand over her mouth.

The two old women are almost giddy. Small towns are weird like that. I'd forgotten what it was like, being a tech worker chained to my desk in Silicon Valley. Now, I'm home. The city needs me.

"Ow!"

Nana swats me. "I said, we're going to the Jingle Bites Café to celebrate, Hughes."

"To pour one out for the deceased," Beryl interrupts.

"Did you know him?"

"Nooo, of course not."

The elderly women snort with laughter behind their hands.

"But it's good to drink to the dead."

"You all will take any excuse to drink." Willow's bubbly red-haired friend smiles.

Willow crosses her arms.

"Why don't you come with us? Willow owns the café," the redhead offers.

"That ownership is in question," I remind them. "Taylor Grace—"

"I don't give a shit what she says," Willow snaps. "And I don't want you in my café anyway."

"Of course she does. She loves men in her café. She'll take them any which way." Beryl grabs my arm.

I don't want to go sit in a café like a pampered pooch. But I need to mine Willow for clues. She's technically the person who found the body.

"There you are!"

Taylor Grace, sobbing, makeup running, stumbles through the crowd, her sister in tow. Lydia has an odd expression on her face. I can't study it, though, because Taylor Grace has thrown herself into my arms.

"My damsel in distress," I murmur.

Willow makes retching noises as Taylor Grace snuggles against my chest.

"You're my favorite person. You're the only one who's on my side, who's on my team. We understand each other, don't we?" She blinks up at me with those striking blue eyes. "You have to promise me. You have to promise me you'll find who murdered Dr. Merriweather. I know Willow killed him." She grabs my jaw. "Prove it to the world."

Then she collapses dramatically in the snow.

"Oh!"

Lydia sighs. "Just leave her."

Her daughter comes over. "Aunt Taylor?"

"It's Aunt Taylor Grace!" my client screams at the little girl.

Lydia grinds her teeth. "Come on. You can—" She sighs again. "Stay at my house tonight, Taylor Grace."

I can't stay and help her. I left my smelling salts at home anyway. My prime suspect is walking away down Main Street. I trail Willow and Josie, listening in on their conversation.

"...think he had to have had enemies, right? Who would want Dr. Merriweather dead?"

"Besides me," Willow mutters.

"I mean, let's be fair. Anyone who gets too close to Taylor Grace gets fucked one way or the other. I should know—hey! Are you eavesdropping?"

"Hoping to overhear a confession."

"Weirdo."

"I think he's cute." Josie giggles.

I flip to a new page in my notepad. "Where were you in the hours before the murder?"

"In the Christmas market. Wait, you're not the cops. I don't have to talk to you." Willow sniffs.

"Worried you'll say the wrong thing and the jig will be up?"

Willow stops short. I almost run into her. She turns on me.

"Are you seriously accusing me of murdering—"

"She was with me all afternoon," Josie interrupts.

"All afternoon?" I press.

"Well..."

"Josie, stop talking."

I scribble on my pad.

"How do we know *you* didn't kill Dr. Merriweather?" Willow demands.

"What? I'm the PI," I remind her. "The private eye is never the murderer. That's not how these things go."

"Yeah, but the jealous lover is."

"The jealous—you think I'm sleeping with my client? That I don't have professional integrity?"

"A private eye is not a profession. Taylor Grace was all over you. You two are sleeping together," Willow says flatly.

"Is she even paying you?" Josie asks.

"I'm doing this out of the goodness of my heart."

"Be prepared to get taken advantage of."

"Sounds like someone's jealous. Could be a motive." I make a note. "Taylor Grace did say you were obsessed with her."

Willow looks hurt.

"I know you killed Dr. Merriweather," I tell her, "and I'm going to prove it."

# CHAPTER 3

## Willow

"He is the fucking worst," I rail to Josie as she samples my latest candy creation: hot cocoa and marshmallow cookies with Peppermint Pattie crumbles.

"You need to sell these," she says, making reaching motions toward the cookies.

I put two on her plate for her.

"I mean, look at him. He's such a weirdo."

"Maybe he's just bored and lonely." Josie pets Lord Mycroft, my guinea pig.

"He could be the murderer," I tell her flatly.

"You think?" Josie pauses and drops the cookie.

Mycroft goes for it, making piggy grunting noises.

"Do not eat that," I scold him and direct him to the greens Hollis brings him from her garden.

Josie picks up the cookie and polishes it off.

"It seems random for him to kill Jonah. I mean, didn't Hughes just get into town? Why kill a random therapist?"

"I don't know. Because he has a personality disorder?"

Hughes is lurking in a corner, his fedora low over his head, the trench coat swishing around him as he surveys the townspeople in my café. Already, several people are looking at me, pointing and whispering. Taylor Grace is bad-mouthing me all over town. I know it.

"Taylor Grace is probably the one who killed Jonah," Josie says.

"Yeah, she would do something like that just to pin it on me because she hates me and wants to ruin my life."

I set two plates of Midnight Snow Cake—dark chocolate sponge with shimmering edible silver dust and snowflake sugar lace—and two cups of our dark roast Christmas Night coffee onto a tray.

Do I really think Taylor Grace killed Dr. Merriweather? I wonder as I head out to the seating area. I mean, I'm not sure I believe that she didn't *not* kill him.

But who else can it be? Aside from Hughes. He might be too incompetent to commit murder. And if he is, the police will figure it out, surely.

"*Don't think anyone will connect it to us...*"

"Orders up!"

"Oh!" The two elderly women jump.

"Talking about the murder?"

"No."

"Yes."

"Just my upcoming ugly-sweater party, Willow. You need to come help us set up. Don't forget."

"And you're making your poinsettia petal cookies, aren't you?" Mary Lou asks me.

"Of course."

"Fabulous. This will be the best party we've had in years."

"Yeah, it's going to top the one when Graham spiked the punch and confessed he was in love with the comptroller's wife." Mary Lou snickers.

"My stove never did work right after he shot it up." Gran slaps the table.

"I need to go see if the police will let me back to my stall," I tell Josie, taking off my apron.

"I should probably go find my child." She looks longingly at the freshly made sugarplum truffles. "Can we trade chocolate for a little help in the shop?"

"Go for it. Though Hollis can come help once she's done with the snow-globe truffles."

"Almost got them, just adding the finishing touch!" my employee calls.

I load up Lord Mycroft into his basket and set out into the wintry night with a broom and some cleaning supplies. The crunch of heavy boots in the snow lets me know I'm not alone.

My lips flatten. "Do you not have a job?"

"This is my—"

"No, I mean a real job."

Hughes's stride lengthens to catch up to me. "I'm retired."

"Bullshit. You're like twelve."

"What?" He stops and grabs my arm. "I'm not twelve. I'm thirty-two."

"You look young."

"I was a computer programmer, and I spent a lot of time inside. Sold my company to Svensson PharmaTech for a lot of money, I might add."

"Ohh, yeah. Now I see why Taylor Grace is obsessed with you."

"She is not. She had a problem she wanted me to solve."

"Aha! The problem being Dr. Merriweather. Murderer." I jab him in the chest.

For a computer programmer, he sure is muscular. Probably a padded suit or something.

"No, you stole from her."

"Wait, you stole from Taylor Grace and murdered her therapist?" one wide-eyed young shopper blurts.

"Yes!" Taylor Grace blows in like a winter storm. A bad one. Not a fun, cozy one that brings holiday cheer.

"I am on the case, Miss Glass," Hughes assures her.

Taylor Grace has already boarded the North Pole Express to Crazy Town.

"The murderess is returning to the scene of the crime. Police! Police! The murderer is here!"

"We don't even know if Dr. Merriweather was actually murdered," Hughes lectures. "The first thing we need is a medical examiner's report to determine—"

Taylor's face contorts into pure hatred and rage. "You don't *believe* me?" she seethes. "You think I'm *lying*? You think I'm *crazy*?" She advances on him like a velociraptor. "You are supposed to be on my side. I need people around me I can trust. She"—Taylor Grace points at me—"murdered Jonah, and you better prove it. Now you come with me. *Now!*" she screams at him.

I almost feel sorry for Hughes as he follows her like a kicked puppy. I know what it's like to be on the receiving end of one of Taylor's tantrums. Serves you right, buddy.

There's caution tape all over my stall. I duck under as I enter. It's a little waterlogged and a little smoky, but the fire department did a fairly good job of not blasting the interior. I'll have to toss all the food, though.

Ugh. More money down the drain.

"Can I have a doughnut, Willow?" Officer Winston Girthman sighs and looks longingly at the display case.

"Sure. Have at it. Take as many as you want. I can't sell them."

Officer Girthman scarfs down an eggnog cream doughnut.

"You want a coffee with that?" I offer.

He nods, chewing.

"Did they get the body off my roof? I guess they don't know what killed him?"

The officer swallows. "Hanging." He pours sugar into his coffee.

"Hanging?" Several of the firemen come in. "Are you freakin' stupid?"

Numbly, I offer them all doughnuts.

"Yeah," Girthman defends himself. "The guy was helping decorate the tree, and he slipped and fell and—accidental hanging. That's what I'm putting in my report."

The firefighters howl with derisive laughter.

"It wasn't an accident."

"He was electrocuted on purpose."

"That's how he died."

"I'm gonna get the medical examiner to look at it when he gets back in town," the police officer counters.

They leave, still arguing.

I'm alone with the carnage. My decorations are in disarray. Everything on the back floating shelves has toppled over. The floor is soggy. I sigh, looking up at the damaged ceiling, and calculate how much money I don't have that it will cost to repair.

Too bad the whole thing didn't just burn down. Then at least I could have gotten a big insurance payout.

Half-heartedly, I start sweeping up, just to do something. Under one of the cases, I hear a metallic ping. Kneeling, I swish with the broom until a small gold earring rolls out from under the case.

I pick it up. Is it a clue? Surely not. But maybe.

I hurry out of the stall to give it to Officer Girthman, but he's disappeared into the crowd of townspeople and tourists gawking at the murder Christmas tree, snapping selfies.

"Winston?" I shout, trying to peer through the crowd.

I shove my way closer to the tree.

"*...have to get paid—*" Gideon Cross's voice carries.

"Why should we pay you? You started a fire in the tree, and someone died," Mayor Loring argues.

"That wasn't me. I didn't do it."

"Still, a man was electrocuted with lights you installed."

"It's the city's lights."

"*Scam!* This whole town is full of liars and scammers."

"And murderers. Though he did bring out the tourists, Meg," Ida remarks. "I see a few fine specimens here, all the way from Manhattan, who might need their Christmas packages unwrapped early."

"I didn't murder nobody. She murdered him!" Gideon yells, pointing at me. "Everyone knows it. She and him was fighting earlier, and she did it to get back at Taylor Grace."

Backing away from the ugly looks of the crowd, I hurry back to the stall.

I have to solve this murder, or Christmas won't just be ruined. It'll be an epic disaster.

# CHAPTER 4

# Hughes

*The office is darker than a fruitcake left in the back of Grandma's pantry. A single strand of Christmas lights blinks in the corner, mocking me with its cheer. I have no leads, no suspects, not even a footprint in the snow—just a body colder than last year's eggnog and a case that smells worse than a candy cane left in a kid's pocket all summer…*

"Hughie!" Nana pokes her head into my bedroom, flinging the door wide open. "Oh, Hughie, you haven't been up all night, have you?"

"I work best in the dark, Nana."

"Well, you're not going to sleep in all day, not in my house." She bustles in and throws open the curtains. "It's the Christmas season, and you can't waste the day. You were raised better than that."

"It's too bright." I wince at the sunlight bouncing off freshly fallen snow.

"There's coffee on the stove."

"It's seven fifteen, Nana."

"It's late. I'd have been up here sooner if I'd known you were already up. Now get dressed." She goes to my closet and starts laying out clothes—Christmas clothes, including a sweater and snow pants.

"I've got my detective uniform."

"It's cold outside." She kisses the top of my head. "I need you to take these invitations for the ugly-sweater party to Mrs. Jones and Mrs. Locke. There are cookie tins, too, with holiday treats for them. I did want to just let you know that Mrs. Locke—her granddaughter just got into town. Now, she's married—"

"Nana—"

"But! I think that she and her husband are on the fritz. You should shoot your shot. You've been working out the past few months." She squeezes my bicep. "You've got money in the bank. You're a good catch. Any woman would be lucky to have you."

"I'm focused on my case, not relationships."

"Hmm." Nana purses her mouth. "There are lots of lonely women out there. 'Tis the season for divorce."

"I don't want to marry a divorcée."

"Of course not. You just need to get a little experience, get your dick wet, then you'll turn all that energy you're wasting on Jonah's accident into finding a nice girl!"

I want to die. "You want me to get with a woman my mom's age?" I complain as she bustles around picking up the empty seltzer cans and my dirty T-shirts. "Nana, I can do it."

"Let me spoil you." She kisses my cheeks. "My little grandbaby, oh, you were such a cute baby, such a chubby little tummy." She pinches my ear hard. "Now, when you do get a girlfriend, don't you leave your dirty undies lying around. You have to clean up after yourself, or she'll leave you."

"I was going to—"

But she's already bustling out.

"Mrs. Cabot tried to sleep with the UPS man, so you have a shot with her!"

"Ugh." I flop back down on the bed and stare at my murder wall of clues.

I have… not that much evidence. Anything I do have is circumstantial.

I stare at Jonah's photo, which I've printed off his website.

"Who killed you and why?"

I spin the case over and over in my head as I sip my coffee from the Santa mug Nana has left out. It's not my aesthetic, but there are no normal dishes in this house. As soon as December hit, everything was replaced with Christmas dishes.

I double-check the addresses on the deliveries then head out into the snow.

Don't tell Nana, but I am slightly regretting my trench coat as I hoof it down the icy sidewalk. The temperature dropped with the incoming snowstorm, and it's freezing.

"Oh! You're Mary Lou's grandson!" A car pulls up.

"Doesn't he look handsome? You did buff up."

"Yeah, I can see the muscles under that thin tarp you're wearing. Don't they have coats in California, boy?"

"Ha ha! Weather's definitely not like here." I'm trying to be nice, but this is the fourth time since I've left Nana's house that someone has stopped to tell me to put on some clothes.

Another car honks at me.

"Hey! Kid, you need a warmer coat!" an old man hollers then skids out and creams a mailbox.

I don't know if Mrs. Locke is awake when I stop at her house.

Her newspaper is at the end of the walkway. I stop to pick it up.

"What are you doing here?"

Taylor Grace's voice comes out of nowhere.

"Uh." I look around wildly.

She's stomping down the sidewalk toward me. "*Uhh*," she mocks. "Why aren't you answering my calls? Why did you send me to voicemail? Are you ignoring me? Huh?"

"It was the middle of the night. I'm trying to work on the case," I say slowly. "What is wrong with you?" The words escape before I can stop them.

"Why do you think something's wrong with me?" Taylor Grace demands. "It sounds like you're trying to accuse me of something. Why? What are you hiding?"

"I'm literally just delivering cookies for my nana, then I'm going to the Christmas market to work on your case."

"Oh!" It's unnerving how her features immediately soften. "Well—" Her arms wrap around my waist. "That's good, isn't it?" She's talking in this baby voice that seemed cute the first time I met her. Now, it's weird.

With how angry she got—and it came on suddenly, like an avalanche on a calm, sunny day—yeah, I guess I could see her being the murderer. I wonder if Willow was onto something after all.

I resist the urge to go home after delivering the last of the cookies.

"I'm living my childhood dream," I whisper to myself, teeth chattering as I walk through the nearly empty Christmas market.

There are only a few influencers wanting to take photos before the crowds swarm for lunch and locals getting in a bit of shopping or restocking their stalls.

"I didn't think dreams would be this cold."

Willow, who wears a knit hat with a red pom-pom low on her head, is stocking her stall.

I grab the top box before it falls off the cart.

"Give that back," she snaps.

"You don't want to say, 'Thanks, Hughes, for saving my expensive merchandise'?" I set the box on the counter.

"Do you want to say, 'Thanks, Willow, for not punching me in the stomach'? Also, where is your coat?"

"Look, I ran into Taylor Grace earlier—"

Willow scoffs.

"No, just hear me out. I'm trying to work on this case, and I do have to explore every angle, right?"

"I'm not a murderer."

"But you have some thoughts on who it could be, right?" I coax.

Willow looks at me with suspicion as she pulls out the little trays of fancy chocolate and starts stocking them in the glass cases. "Thoughts? So now you want me to do your job for you?"

I blow out a breath. It hovers in front of me. "Look, I'm not trying to be your friend, but Taylor Grace is getting a little unhinged about this murder, okay? She is really bent out of shape about Jonah's death. This is going to sound crazy, but I don't think she's sleeping. She's been acting paranoid and almost possessed."

Willow doesn't look shocked or concerned. She just starts laughing. "Whooo! She finally split on ya, huh? Well, you lay down with backstabbing bitches, prepare to get fleas."

"Look, I think she might literally kill me if we don't solve this murder."

"We? Who?" Willow scoffs.

"Just we, the collective? Also, right now, you're my only suspect."

And maybe Taylor Grace, but it's sacrilegious to say that about my client.

"Really, I'm your only suspect?" Willow slams the glass case's door shut. "What about Jonah's wife, Lenore? What about Damien, Taylor Grace's boyfriend? Shit, what about Gideon Cross? Did you look into him?"

"You really think one of them could have done it? I mean, sure, I'll look into the wife, but what motive would Gideon or Damien have?" I argue.

"The fact that Taylor Grace was sleeping with Jonah?"

"No way."

"Dude, I know Taylor Grace way better than you. I would be shocked if she wasn't sleeping with him, and if you think because she's sleeping with you that she wouldn't cheat—"

"She's not sleeping with me."

Willow makes a noise like she doesn't believe me.

"Women she tries to turn into her bosom friends—to paraphrase *Anne of Green Gables*—and men she wants to turn into her daddy or her boyfriend. Probably both. Anyways, since you and the police are completely incompetent, apparently, I'll have to go solve this murder."

"You aren't a licensed PI," I protest.

"I'm going to talk to Gideon."

"You're just going to accost him? What if you spook him?" I argue, rushing after her.

"I'm not. I'm delivering his mail."

"Me too."

"No, you're not." She glares over her shoulder. "Go do your own investigation."

# CHAPTER 5

## Willow

Hughes follows me through the town square and around the murder tree to Gideon Cross's stall. There's still that unnerving smell of barbecue in the air. Gideon must have fixed the lights, though, because the tree glows merrily. Someone's added a bow to cover up the bald spot where the body was.

"How can he afford a stall this close to the tree?" Hughes asks in a low voice.

"He inherited it, I think, like I did."

"Who'd you inherit your stall from?"

"My dad inherited it from his grandfather. It's not free, though. You still have to pay the fees. There's a waiting list for my spot," I explain.

The lights are on in Gideon's stall. I loved this stall when I was a kid, with all the tiny train sets chugging along through the miniature town. I would always go visit Gideon's great-uncle, who used to run it.

Now? The stall looks a little worn and tired. The miniature trains, trees, and little houses for sale for a train set at home are dusty with faded labels, like no one's been buying them.

The train chugs around the track, but the village hasn't been set up with as much care as when Gideon's late great-uncle did it.

"Gideon!" I call. "Hello?"

I walk into the stall.

The lights on the main Christmas tree were oversized, but the ones wrapped around Dr. Merriweather—they were different, weren't they? Shoot, I need to see some crime scene photos.

"Did you take photos of the corpse?" I ask Hughes, voice lowered.

"What?"

I point at the lights festooned around the tiny village.

He nods, pulls out his phone, and zooms in on the lights wrapped around Dr. Merriweather's fried arm. They look very similar.

"Could be the same lights—"

"*What are you doing in here?*"

We jump.

Hughes jostles one of the little houses, and he curses as he sets it back in place.

"Hey, Gideon. Just delivering some mail that got mixed up with mine." I wave the envelopes.

He snatches them from me without even saying thank you. "It's just junk mail," Gideon mutters and dumps them in the small trash can next to the ancient cash register.

"So, has business picked up for you since the murder?" I rock in my boots.

"Why, you after my stall too?" he snaps.

"What, me? No, I can barely take care of my own. Just trying to get a little solidarity going with a fellow stall owner affected by the tragedy."

"Not a tragedy. This town is better off without Jonah Merriweather." Gideon scowls.

"What makes you say that?" Hughes asks.

Gideon just glares at him.

"You and Taylor Grace aren't going to pin his death on me!" he hollers. "Get out! Out! I'm not the only one who hated Jonah Merriweather. You need to leave me and my shop alone!"

"Well, that went better than expected," I say when we're back in the Christmas market.

"I'll say." Hughes whistles and pulls out a stack of mail.

"Where did you get that? Did you steal that? What kind of PI are you?" I hiss.

"The kind who solves cases." Hughes grins.

"Oh my gosh."

"Do you want to know what's in them or not?" He waves the mail at me.

In my stall, Hughes takes out a knife and slices open the top envelope on the stack of mail.

"What is it?"

"A late notice." He frowns. "Credit card bill due. Rent due."

"So he's prickly because he can't pay his bills."

"Maybe. He should start charging for photos if he's worried about cash." Hughes nods to several girls taking photos in front of the stall. "I mean—" He shows me an Instagram feed. "People literally come to this town just to visit his stall and don't buy anything."

"Yeah, but what does that have to do with the murder?" I cross my arms.

Hughes shrugs. "Maybe Jonah wanted that stall spot?" he muses.

"To run his therapy stand? It doesn't make any sense. It's a dead end," I argue.

"But the lights match," Hughes reminds me.

"Might match. Anyways, this is a waste of time," I huff. "Thanks for nothing."

"*Traitor!*" someone shrieks. "*You're a stain on this Christmas market!*"

# CHAPTER 6

# Hughes

"Taylor Grace incoming." Willow sags as my client storms across the town square, tourists skittering out of her way.

"Did something happen with Gideon?" I ask Taylor, putting myself between her and Willow, hoping to get some usable information before she spirals into her Willow obsession.

"He's going behind my back with her," Taylor rages. "They're both trying to cut me out of the company. They're going to team up and go into business together."

"No, we're not." Willow is incredulous.

I'm experiencing whiplash.

"They're plotting against me," Taylor fumed. "Willow stole Gideon from me like she stole my business, and now, they're going to team up and take over the Christmas market."

"I sell chocolate, not trains," Willow argues.

"You have to believe me, Hughie," Taylor sobs, turning on the waterworks like she's just hit a button. "Only Jonah believed me. I wish he weren't dead. I don't know what I'm going to do. How will I survive?" she wails.

"Don't fucking listen to her." A man in a heavy coat and workman's boots stomps through the snow. "She's a lying, crazy bitch."

"Help me!" Taylor Grace hides behind me, grabbing my coat, tearing it open so the wind whips through. "Help me, Hughes. You're my only hope. He's going to kill me like he killed Jonah."

"I thought you said Willow killed Jonah," I remind her, tugging the coat closed, trying not to shiver.

"I don't know who killed him!" Taylor screams at me. "*I* don't *know*. That's not my *job* to figure it out."

"Yeah, it's just your job to lie about your husband." Damien clenches his fists.

I don't even like Damien, and I feel sorry for him.

"She's been telling everyone she wants a divorce because my dick's too small. Is my dick small, Willow? You've seen it," Damien demands.

"You're sleeping with Taylor's husband?" I ask Willow, shocked.

"She is?" Taylor is too surprised to be angry.

"No!" Willow hollers. "Damien's a creep and went streaking at our high school graduation."

"And it wasn't small, was it?" Damien smirks.

"I never said that," Taylor Grace pouts.

"Ida says you did." Damien gears up for an argument.

"I was just repeating what Willow said." Taylor Grace tosses her hair.

"I don't care how big your lazy husband's dick is or how bad he is in bed," Willow argues.

"I'm not bad. I'm great. This chick is crazy." Damien jerks a thumb at Taylor Grace.

"You're crazy. Jonah says you're bad for me." Taylor Grace waves her arms.

"Yeah, Jonah. All you talk about is Jonah. That man was a fraud. He ruined my marriage. He's the reason you want a divorce," Damien rails.

"I'm going down to city hall to get a restraining order against you. I'm going to make sure you spend Christmas in jail." Taylor grabs her purse.

"Yeah, right."

The two rush off.

"You know what I'm starting to think?" I say slowly as I wait for my ears to stop ringing. "I think you're correct, Willow, and Taylor Grace is the murderer."

"Oh, Taylor wouldn't kill anyone."

Hollis—I think her name is—worms into the stall with a rack of maple bacon doughnuts.

"She was shitty to you too," Willow says.

Hollis sighs and sets the box of doughnuts on the counter.

"She had a traumatic childhood. She can't help it." Hollis is more sympathetic than I'm willing to be. "Now, yesterday, Josie wanted me to make more of these marshmallow cookies. They're in this bottom box. She thinks they're going to be a hit. I posted them on our socials already. There's a ton of interest!"

"Hopefully, Taylor Grace doesn't show up to ruin the launch." Willow massages her temples. "We need to sell out. Stall dues are due Saturday."

Hollis looks at me. "No progress?"

"Of course he hasn't made any progress. He's a useless male playing dress-up," Willow snorts.

"Hey! I'm going to solve this thing. Just you watch." I swat her with my hat.

"It's always the lover or the spouse who killed them, right?" Hollis giggles. "I mean, I hate true crime podcasts. I like cozy mysteries myself, but, like, isn't it usually the most obvious answer?"

"Sometimes," I start to lecture, "though, with the rate of unsolved murders being 50 percent, I believe a statistically significant number of victims are murdered by complete strangers."

"We'd know if someone new came into town," Hollis argues.

"There are all the tourists."

"Someone could have come into town and slipped out, Willow," I remind her.

"Fun. Well, I'll let you sit here and mansplain murder while I go actually solve this. Hollis, can you man the stand for a bit? Shouldn't be much traffic," Willow tells her as she packs cookies in a box.

"Sure. Are you going back to the store? Could you take the boxes back?"

"I will, but I'm going to the police station first."

"The police! Did you figure out who killed Jonah?"

"No, but I'm going to solve it. I cannot take the entirety of the Christmas season with Taylor Grace and her flying monkeys ruining the holidays. I need to know everything the police do."

"You need me to come with you." I put on my hat. "I've spent the last few months buttering up the officers. We're all friends."

I take the box from Willow. She has to hurry to keep up with my long legs. She's kind of cute, huffing along beside me.

"So, you just follow my lead here. I'm used to dealing with cops."

"And I went to preschool with these jokers. I don't need your help solving this murder case. You had no suspects, and now I have several viable ones."

"I had suspects, but I'm not solving this case on vibes. I'm doing it on facts."

"And the facts are that we need more evidence before we can put any of these men on the suspect list."

"But I'm on the suspect list," she counters.

"You're not *not* on the suspect list."

"You're going to throw a tantrum when I solve this case before you, aren't you?"

The police officers are all standing around when we walk into the police station, passing several elderly people sleeping off their eggnog in the drunk tank.

"We brought cookies, boys! New recipe!" Willow calls.

"Hughes." Officer Girthman trudges over.

Bobby greedily takes two cookies. "Delicious. I saw these on Instagram. So good," he says around the crumbs.

"Yeah, it's a new recipe. Hopefully, everyone likes it."

I can't take any more of the small-town small talk. I need answers. I cut in. "Now, Bobby, look. A man's been murdered, and we need some information."

Bobby squirms.

"This is a high-profile case. The mayor didn't like it when we said it would be ruled an accident. I can't just be giving out evidence."

"We don't want evidence, just a little information," Willow presses.

"We can leave her out of it. She doesn't have to know."

"Well—"

Willow tries to shove me aside. "Bobby, you tell me the information. I made you cookies," she wheedles. "You like them, don't you? I'm making extra-special cookies every day this month. You can have one of each."

"I can?"

"And I'll give you that peppermint tea you like so much too."

He perks up. "Well, we don't really have any information." He hands me a folder.

"What's this?"

"That's our evidence."

"This is your evidence?"

"His clothes, all burnt up."

"What about his phone?" I demand. "I know computers. I can recover data as an assist to the department."

"No phone. We didn't find one on him."

"Did you check under the tree?"

"Yeah, I did," he whines. "The mayor made us."

"Great detective work," Willow says dryly.

"When can I get my cookies?" he asks hopefully.

"You didn't give us anything useful, Bobby. You're not getting cookies."

"But—"

"You know where to find me if you have something."

"*Call me,*" I mouth over my shoulder as I trail an angry Willow out of the station.

I try to look tough and not shiver beside her on the street while Willow paces angrily.

"Well, shoot. That phone is probably with the murderer." She turns to me. "You're a computer wiz. Track it and find it, and let's solve this thing."

"I can't do that. That's not how computers work. I'm not a wizard."

"Really? Don't virgins turn into wizards at age thirty?"

"It's age forty, which I'm not. And I'm not a virgin," I snap.

Several people look at me askance.

I lower my voice. "I have had sex before."

Willow slow claps. "Good for you."

"And I'm going to have it again."

"With Mrs. Cabot?"

I don't like her shit-eating grin. I step back.

"Be careful. My granny claims she gave everyone at the yacht club gonorrhea. Also, crap." She turns and heads back into the station.

"What are you—"

"Hey, Bobby! Let Gran out of the cell, please."

Bobby shuffles.

"Bobby," she warns. "*Now.* I have things to do today, and I'm not coming back down here by the time you actually process her."

"You have to pay bail."

"Do you want me to rescind the invite to her ugly-sweater party?"

"Can I have a cookie?"

Willow sighs and hands over the box.

His keys jingle as he opens the cell door.

Her grandmother, Beryl, yawns and smacks her lips. "Partied a little too hard." She winks at me. "Ding-dong, Jonah is dead," she hums.

# CHAPTER 7

# Willow

I text Josie after I drop Gran off at her house with instructions to please take a shower.

**Willow:** *Hey wanted to see if you wanted to hang out and talk through this murder investigation?*
**Willow:** *Can't believe I'm writing those words.*
**Willow:** *This year has truly been the worst.*
**Josie:** *I'm busy with the kids but I'll stop by your stall a little later ok?*
**Josie:** *I promise we'll hang later! Save me some of those cookies!*

I blink back tears.

It's just the cold wind. I mulishly wipe at them with a gloved hand.

On the cold, snowy street, I feel about as lonely as I ever have.

That was how Taylor Grace got me. Josie and I used to be best friends—we still are—but she got a handsome, rich boyfriend, then got married, then had a baby, and I barely texted her anymore, let alone saw her. Taylor Grace had been on the periphery of my social circle for years. She seemed fun and cool, and when Josie had less and less time for me, I started hanging out with Taylor Grace.

It was like we were kindred spirits. Friendship soulmates. We liked the same music and loved baking and the town of Harrogate.

In hindsight, she was just toxic and pretending to be my friend. I ignored all the little criticisms, the digs about my weight, about my family.

She would always tell me to stop texting Josie so much, to stop asking her to hang out, that I was annoying her, that I was bothering her. Then she would hug me and say, "But don't worry, we're best friends."

As if.

I never should have gone into business with her. We didn't have a formal contract, so I thought I was protected. But Taylor Grace is bad-mouthing me around town, saying I stole her business.

*Too bad she wasn't the one who died.*

"Now that's an awful thing to think," I scold myself as I head back into the Christmas market.

People are staring at me.

"What the—"

"You're the murderer!" several tween girls scream dramatically and run away.

A couple of the maintenance staff from the city give me odd looks.

"What?" I snap at one of them.

"Is that you on the poster?" he blurts.

"The—" I whirl around.

On a stall, a flyer is tacked up.

*WANTED: MURDERER!*

***Do NOT patronize the Jingle Bites Café, or you are supporting a MURDERER!!!!***

"Is there really a warrant out for your arrest?"

"Is this reward real?"

I tear down the poster.

"No. It's not."

Taylor fucking Grace.

I need to find the killer stat. But I don't have any clues. The police are useless. Well, actually… I do have one clue. The earring is where I left it at the bottom of the cash drawer. I pocket it as several people approach the stall.

"Do you have cookies left?" one tourist asks. "The ones from Instagram?"

I hate Christmas.

"Of course!" I am really digging deep to sound cheery.

"I need two of them. The prettiest ones."

Hollis shows up as the girls film themselves holding up the cookies, photographing the cookies in front of the tree, taking a single bite of each cookie, and making orgasm noises.

"I raised the prices on the cookies," Hollis whispers to me and winks. "Christmas surcharge."

"Oh! I couldn't figure out if something was wrong with the system!"

"We need to fix that roof, right?" Hollis grins.

The tourists chuck the cookies, each of which has a single bite taken out of it, into the trash can.

I want to scream then keel over in the snow and not wake up until after Valentine's Day.

Hollis must have seen something on my face because she whispers, "Why don't you take a breather? I'll deal with things here."

I try to emotionally reregulate as I meander through the stalls. The jewelry stalls tend to cluster near the historic city hall building. I head slowly in that direction, taking a few moments to stop and survey the Christmas stalls.

Two men on horseback—the Christmas market security—are parked right outside one of the stalls. A horse snorts and turns his head toward me.

"On behalf of the Christmas market committee, we are issuing a citation," one of the men states.

"You're what?" the stall owner complains. "I have a right to sell my products!"

"You can't sell candles. You've only been permitted to sell fine jewelry and some jewelry-inspired ornaments, Ruby. The Christmas committee doesn't want the market flooded with people selling candles. We need variety in the Christmas market."

"I could sell candles last year," Ruby complains as one of the Christmas cops hands her a box and she starts packing away the candles. "As long as it's Christmas themed, we're allowed to sell it. Those were the rules last year."

"We're tightening things up."

"It's because of Jonah, isn't it?" Ruby demands.

"RIP, but the mayor agrees with him on this."

Hmm. Another suspect?

Seems no one except Taylor Grace liked Jonah.

I duck into a random jewelry stall nearby and almost crash into—

Yup.

Hughes.

His dark eyes narrow when he sees me. "I thought you were working."

"Shopping for your girlfriend?" I counter.

"You have a girlfriend?" the woman behind the counter squeals. "Oh, Mary Lou will be so excited. Is this her?" She points at me. "You're dating Willow?"

"Barf. God, no." I make a face.

"Aw, you'd make a cute couple." She giggles. "And Willow is a minor town celebrity."

"Thanks to the murder?" Hughes raises an eyebrow.

I kick him.

"Oh!" The jeweler giggles. "You two are so cute. Willow's going to win the town baking competition. You should have won last year, dear. Those chocolate-covered marshmallow caramel bites were divine. That sprinkle of sea salt. Better than sex. You should give him one."

Hughes looks down at me.

"And make him wear a coat," she adds.

Hughes follows me out. "You're investigating, aren't you?"

It's not lost on me how he pulls the thin trench coat around him. "Guess women aren't the only ones who sacrifice comfort for fashion."

"I'm not cold," he says stubbornly as he follows me deeper into the market. "What are you investigating? Did you find another clue?"

"And you're buying things for Taylor Grace, aren't you?"

"No. For my mom."

"Hmm."

"You don't believe me?"

"Men are liars."

"Wow."

I should tell him to fuck off, but I don't really have the patience to deal with tourists, and between Taylor Grace being a malevolent Christmas spirit and Josie being busy, well, it is nice to have someone to talk to. Argue with, I mean.

"Okay, fine." I pull out the earring. "I found this in my stall after Dr. Merriweather, you know, ate his last Christmas cookie."

He picks it up off my palm, inspecting the earring.

"How do you know it was there from the murderer?"

"I don't," I admit. "But if you have better clues to follow up on, I'm all ears."

"No. The police haven't been much help."

"Shocker."

He follows me into a stall that sells higher-end Christmas-themed gold jewelry.

"Looking for something special?" the middle-aged woman asks from behind the counter.

"Maybe—" I pull out the earring. "Do you sell anything that looks like this?"

"Hmmm." She inspects it.

"This looks like a design I sold a ton of a couple of years ago. I'm off this design, though. You always have to have new things at the Christmas market."

"Shoot. I guess you don't remember who bought them?"

She gives me a weird look.

"My fiancée likes them so much," Hughes jumps in, "that we are thinking about giving them as bridal party favors." His arm slides around my waist.

I smile like I'm part of a happy couple.

"But I warned her that we need to check and make sure the girls don't already have duplicates. And it's not like she can just snoop in their houses, especially because a lot of them live out of town."

"Oh!" The woman brightens. "I love a wedding! What a fun gift. Let me pull my records."

Hughes winks at me.

She hums along to the jazzy tune of "Rudolph the Red-Nosed Reindeer" coming from the speakers.

"This system is so hard to work." She sighs, peering through her glasses at the iPad.

"May I?"

"He's a computer wiz," I tell her. "He sold his company to Svensson PharmaTech for big bucks."

"Oh! And now you're making him pay you back for a nice wedding after he worked all those long hours away from home, aren't you?" She winks.

"He's definitely going to pay, all right." I grind my teeth.

"Got the list." Hughes hits a button, and the list prints on the receipt paper.

"Well, aren't you clever?" She claps her hands.

"Not clever enough to wear a warm coat," I mutter.

"Well, I think you look very handsome." The jeweler smooths down the lapels.

"Thank you, ma'am." He tips his fedora and everything.

"Seriously?" I hiss at him when we're out of sight of the stall. "Your fiancée?"

"Hey, who got you that list?"

"I could have gotten it."

"No, you couldn't." A smile plays around his soft, dumb mouth. "You needed a man to get that information for you. She wasn't going to hand it over. You don't look trustworthy."

"I'm trustworthy!"

He points at one of Taylor Grace's signs.

I tear it down and stuff it into an elf-shaped trash can.

It shrieks, "Merry Christmas!" at me.

"So, should I throw out the list…?" He waves it in my direction.

"No!" I snatch it from him.

He peers over my shoulder.

I expect him to smell like stale coffee and cigarettes for some reason, but instead, he smells crisp and fresh, like walking through an abandoned Christmas tree farm on a winter afternoon.

"I don't see anyone I recognize on our suspect list."

"I don't know most of these people. Gran probably will." I pocket the list and turn, but he's right there. I look up at him. "You can go now."

He stares down at me. "You can't kick me out when the investigation's getting good."

"It's not getting anywhere. I have to go buy some stuff for Gran's party."

"I'll come too. I can help you carry it. I have to go back to Juniper Avenue in a little bit anyway. Nana's expecting a delivery."

I'm not taking him up on that offer, right? I grab the lapels of his trench coat. "Hopefully, you'll get a real coat while you're there. The temperature is supposed to drop."

He briefly wraps his arms around me. "Or maybe I can just keep you to warm me up."

# CHAPTER 8

# Hughes

I don't know why I hugged her. Probably because I'm terrible and awkward at flirting.

Willow looks at me like I have three heads.

I laugh, trying to play it off as a joke as I release her. "You can't tell me you don't think I look great in the trench coat."

"At least you're not wearing it with sweatpants." Her eyes slide down my body to my boots. "At least I assume there aren't sweatpants under there."

"I'd open this up and show you, but I'm actually very close to freezing to death here."

"I knew it!" she crows. "I knew you were cold. The Trekhaven is on First Avenue. They have warm coats."

"My nana bought me a coat, but it's bright red," I complain to her. "And it has a matching hood. I'll look like ski patrol."

"Then buy your own coat, asshole." She laughs.

"You don't know my nana. If I show up in a new coat, I'll never hear the end of it."

"Oh my gosh."

"Oh come on, if your granny bought you a gift and then you went out and bought an identical one, she'd be ticked," I protest.

"No, actually, I think she'd be very happy if I came home with a new sex toy."

I double over laughing. "Stop, you're pulling my leg. Your own grandmother bought you a sex toy?"

"Shh!" She giggles. "Not so loud, this is a family-friendly event."

"What kind of sex toy? I mean, like, what does that even mean? Like a dildo?"

"Yeah, it's called Santa's Beast and—"

I collapse, hand over my mouth, against a speaker pole. "You're lying!" I grab her arm, and she hauls me up. "You're lying. That's horrible."

"I know, right?"

I almost—*almost*—ask her if she's actually used it, but that would be really awkward.

"Ah, young love. How revolting."

"Lilith, heyyy!" Willow waves to a pale-skinned young woman with long raven black hair and dark, soulless eyes.

I shiver, and not from my poor clothing choices.

Lilith's dark eyes bore into mine for an excruciatingly long moment, then she turns back to her customer. "Steep these leaves for five minutes in boiling water," she instructs, handing over a sachet of parchment paper.

I stare at the older woman.

Lenore Merriweather.

"Hi, Mrs. Merriweather. I'm so sorry for your loss," Willow says, going in for a hug, thinking better of it, then patting Lenore awkwardly on the shoulder. "Gran is making quiche lorraine for you."

The widow stares at Willow. Her face is splotchy and red. She looks like she's about to faint. "I hate quiche." Then, silently, she turns and hurries away.

Willow tugs on her sweater collar.

Next to me, a black cat seems to materialize out of nowhere and meows loudly.

"Next customer."

"I need to pick up the mulled wine spice order. For the Christmas party," Willow says. "Are you coming?"

"I hate Christmas."

"There will be a bonfire." Willow rocks on her heels.

A large burlap sack lands on the rough wood counter with a thud. I dutifully pick it up. The sharp scent of the spices tickles my nose.

"What, ah, how's Lenore doing?" Willow winces.

"How should I know? We're not friends." Lilith takes the money Willow hands her. "I did offer her 20 percent off a Ouija board session to talk to her deceased husband."

"Very generous of you."

"We do what we can for our neighbors."

"She didn't say anything at all to you about who she thinks killed him?" Willow prods.

"Maybe she'll say more at the funeral."

"Are you going?" I ask. "I thought you weren't friends."

"Any excuse to attend a funeral." She gives me a sharp smile.

"We'll see you there, then."

Willow and I race out of the spooky stall.

I look around outside. The fog from earlier is clearing. I'm turned around. "Wait." I whirl.

It's like the stall vanished. I stifle a curse.

"Guess we can cross Lenore off the list," Willow says, chewing her bottom lip.

"Her grief could just be a ruse," I argue. "We need to see how much she benefits from his death, if she was cheating on him, you know. I mean, the man died, what, less than twenty-four hours ago, and she's out about town, doing her Christmas shopping? It's suspicious."

I shift the heavy bag, watching as Willow stares at my arms.

"Don't worry, I won't drop it."

"*Just leave it, Taylor Grace. She doesn't want to,*" someone declares loudly.

I take off after Willow to a small seating area decorated with garlands. It would be picturesque, the perfect cozy pocket away from the holiday madness of the Christmas market—except that there are several screaming children, an exasperated pregnant woman, a drunk husband, and of course, Taylor Grace.

"She really is crazy."

"You're just figuring that out?"

Willow and I huddle next to a large snowman sandwich signboard.

"I'm her auntie." Taylor Grace tugs at the five-year-old girl having a tantrum on the ground. "She wants to go shopping with me. Make her stop crying!"

"For God's sake, Lydia, do something about your crazy sister," Travis demands, hand over his phone.

"This is why I didn't want to have kids with you," Damien says loudly, stomping up. "And you better keep an eye on her," he tells Lydia, who's trying to wrangle her kids while her husband complains to someone on the phone. "I bet Taylor's having an affair with him." He points at Travis.

"You never support me," Taylor Grace sobs to her sister. "Everyone likes you better than me. It's always 'How can we help Lydia?' 'What can we do to make Lydia's life easier?' No one ever takes care of me."

"What about your creepy PI?" Lydia's husband snaps, covering the phone speaker.

"Shoot."

"Hughes!" Taylor rushes over to me.

"Hey, just, uh, was getting stuff for the Christmas party."

"Oh, of course." Her face screws up when she sees Willow. "Of course you're sneaking around behind my back." Her tone has this angry, hysterical edge. "You of all people. You can't buy loyalty these days, apparently."

Willow stands next to me, her mouth a thin line, like she's struggling not to say anything.

"And you, you're always trying to steal people's things," Taylor spits. "You're trying to steal my man like you stole my company. Well, guess what? His penis doesn't belong to you. It belongs to me."

"What the—" I'm shocked.

"Taylor Grace!" Lydia claps her hands over her kids' ears. "Can you watch your language?"

"Maybe you need to do a better job of being a mother. I can't be expected to police what I'm saying," her sister snaps.

"She's not coming to Christmas if she acts like that!" Travis bellows.

"I have to go." Willow grabs the sack of herb mix.

I watch her run off while Taylor Grace has a complete meltdown in the Christmas market. Yeah, Taylor definitely could have killed Dr. Merriweather. I need to find a way to talk to Lenore.

# CHAPTER 9

## Willow

I wish Josie were here. I want to talk to someone about whatever the hell that was.

The bag in my arms is heavy.

I wish I'd let Hughes take it home for me. The way the muscles under that stupid trench coat bulged. Who knew he was that buff underneath that dumb private eye costume?

My stall is dark. There's a Be Right Back! sign on the rope crossing the entrance.

I blow out a breath and stand there, trying to decide if I want to set the bag down in the snow so I can undo the rope or if I want to walk five steps to set the bag on a nearby bench.

There's rustling in the stall.

"What the...?"

A dark figure ducks under the rope and rushes past me, almost knocking the bag out of my arms.

"Hey!" I yell after the figure. "*Hey!*"

I dump the bag on the bench next to a confused tourist. "Did you see who was in my stall?"

"No." She goes back to looking at pictures of cats in elf outfits on her phone.

"What the hell?"

I flip on the lights in the stall.

"Hollis?" I call.

I check my phone. There's a missed call and a text message from Hollis.

> **Hollis:** *I have to step away for a minute, back to the cafe! Apparently, Rose left to go see her boyfriend. *grimace emoji* Left a sign up on the stall.*

"Maybe that was her," I wonder as I retrieve the spiced wine mix.

At least I don't see anything missing from the stall. But I don't believe that was Hollis—there's no way she would run past me like that without saying hello.

I hear something jostle behind me.

Is it the intruder?

"Josie!"

"Hi!" My friend hugs me. "Finally got away from the kids. Oh! Are those the peanut butter truffles?"

"Sure, you can have one." I roll my eyes but can't help grinning at my friend.

"Is this the wine mix for the party? You can't let me drink too much," Josie warns.

"You're coming still?"

"Yeah, duh," she says around the gooey truffle. "I never miss your granny's party. I already told Mace he has to watch the baby."

"Mace can come, too, if he wants," I tell her, trying not to be the possessive friend. I can hear Taylor Grace in my head.

"He's not a big party person anyway. Though maybe I'll get him to come out. Whoo! Par-tay! It's going to be epic. I'll come early to help set up, and also you have to tell me which ugly sweater you think is best. I have one that says, 'I'm a ho ho ho,' but maybe that's more trashy than ugly."

She chatters as I fill orders for people, carefully wrapping up gift boxes of truffles.

"Speaking of trashy, any progress on the murder?" She looks excited.

"Not much." I fill her in on the earring, the phone, and Lenore.

"That's progress," she says. "Baby steps."

"I don't have time to make baby steps." I show her one of Taylor Grace's flyers. "She's trying to ruin me. She wants to steal the business, and she's trying to get me arrested. She's batshit insane!"

"We need to find that phone. The murderer clearly took it." I glance around. "I don't even know where to start looking."

"The scene of the crime. No, I mean the *scene of the crime*." She makes porno-music noises and gyrates her hips.

"Oh, barf, gross, *blech*."

"We need to sneak into Dr. Merriweather's office. The police must have missed some clues there."

"Yeah, just let me see if I can get Hollis back over here to—Rose! Hey!" I wave.

"Hollis sent me over to help." The teenager touches up her lip gloss. "You really should hire another person."

"Yeah, if Taylor Grace hadn't burned through our financial reserves chasing stupid product ideas, I might be able to. Thanks, Rose."

She's bouncing up and down.

"If you want your boyfriend here, then he needs to help."

Josie links arms with me, skipping along next to me through the Christmas market.

"I also told Mace I'm going to be out tomorrow afternoon and to make arrangements. I need to make sure I can fit in my little black dress."

"You're going out?"

"To the funeral."

"The what? We can't go to the funeral."

"We need to look for clues. I'm addicted to your candy. I can't have Taylor Grace shutting you down because she's jealous and crazy. I'm a sugar addict."

"Okay, soooo…"

We stare up at Dr. Merriweather's office in the middle of the block on Fourth Street. The sounds of the Christmas market are a dull murmur.

Josie grins. "Let's do a little breaking and entering."

"Oh my god, we're going to get arrested." I tug half-heartedly at the door with Dr. Merriweather Psychiatry etched on it in faded gold lettering. "It's locked. Too bad."

"You give up too easily."

"What are we, breaking the glass? We need a key, or—" I look up at the window above me. "A monkey?"

"Nope, we're going through the window. And right on schedule."

She beams at three little blond boys, who toddle up, trailed by a surly teenager, nose buried in his phone. He grunts in greeting. The triplets dance around Josie as she claps her hands.

"Hellooo! Hello! Hi!"

"Hi!" they squeal. Then they turn to me. "Hi!" They surround me, hugging my legs.

My heart melts.

Part of me wished I could have kids like Josie. But I don't have a steady job or a business. I live in the shed in the back of my granny's house, and I'm surrounded by crazy people. So…

I really need Santa to bring me debt relief, not a baby for Christmas.

"Can you boys get up there?" Josie points at the window.

"Yeah." They nod. "Yeah, yeah, we got it."

I frown then look at the teenage brother. "Hey, Calvin, is this normal?"

He shrugs. "Crawford just took the triplets to Boston with him to break into someone's house, so I guess Josie can do it too."

The triplets have already shucked their shoes and socks and are scampering up the drainpipe to the window.

"That's it, there you go! Yep, crowbar that up. Whoo, they're in!"

In half a second, the boys have scampered down the stairs. One jumped on the other's shoulders so he could flip the dead bolts.

"And we're in!" Josie whoops. "Nice!" They slap her a high five.

I hold out my hand for a high five as well.

"There better be money in that fist bump, lady."

"Oh, you!" Josie pokes one boy in his round little belly.

He giggles.

"Here." She hands them several twenties.

The teen perks up.

"Stole it from Mace's wallet. Shhh. Go nuts, but don't spend it all in one place." She puts a finger against her lips. "I love being a detective! Maybe I should get a fun hat like your handsome private eye." Josie winks.

"He's not handsome."

"Mm-hm, those arms, and I bet he has a nice butt under that trench coat. You should unwrap him like a present and find out."

I creep up the stairs behind Josie. She's walking like she owns the place—which I guess she does. If we get arrested, her husband's brother is married to the mayor, and his other brother regularly sends bribes to the police. Not to mention her husband owns the factory that basically keeps this town running.

Me? My gran is a regular in the drunk tank, so maybe I'm not too bad off. But still. I can't afford to be away from Jingle Bites, not when we're so understaffed.

Josie and I walk into the musty office. It's like stepping back in time to the seventies.

"Guess Jonah never updated after his dad retired." Josie looks around at the wood paneling on the walls.

Dust motes float through the chilly air. On one shelf sits a photo of a man with a miniature train. Next to the photo is a bare patch of empty shelf, like something's been moved.

"Jonah's late father." I snap a few photos. Then I thumb through the lawbooks, trying to see if he has anything hidden in them.

Josie opens desk drawers and rifles through papers.

"Anything?"

"Take a look at this," she says.

We sit on the couch.

"Divorce papers."

"Was he filing?"

"Yep. Cites irreconcilable differences, dead bedroom, claims Lenore disrespected him. I don't think he filed these." She shows me the Post-it. "I think his lawyer told him that it's probably not a good idea to air all your dirty laundry in court like that."

"So she didn't know. If she knew, then I'd say that's motive."

"She could have found the papers or seen something on his phone, or he could have verbally told her, so his wife killed him. Then, instead of everything fifty-fifty, she would get it all."

I sit back on the couch, rubbing my face. "We don't have anything concrete."

"Don't speak too soon." Josie reaches next to my arm and digs out a scrap of pink fabric wedged between the couch seat cushions.

We stare at the panties.

"I think these are too small for Lenore."

"The perfect size for Taylor Grace." I poke them with a pen. "How did the police miss these?"

"Full of nepo hires. Apparently, the Svenssons like it that way because they don't want smart cops looking into their business." Josie shrugs.

The front door slams. Then a current of cold air flows up the stairs.

We freeze.

Heavy male footsteps ascend the old wooden steps.

We look around wildly. Where are we going to hide?

## CHAPTER 10

# Hughes

*It's a dark afternoon. I'm no closer to solving the case than I was the day Dr. Merriweather died, even after trekking down to the city hall to sweet-talk the kind little old lady at the counter into giving me all of the complaints lodged by Dr. Merriweather against these small-town residents.*

*My feet carry me to his office. But someone's been here before me. The place is probably ransacked.*

*The door is ajar—like a bad present half wrapped, begging to be opened. I pushed it inward slowly, and the hinges creak like an old carol sung off-key. The lobby smells of pine cleaner and stale peppermint schnapps. A sad little tree slumps in the corner, its lights blinking like a guilty conscience.*

*The stairs loom ahead—narrow, steep, the kind of stairs that whisper secrets when you climb them. I take them one at a time, my hand brushing the banister, which is sticky from forgotten candy cane fingers. Each step is a drumbeat, each creak a warning....*

I hear someone up there. Is it the murderer returning to the scene of the crime?

I reach for my gun.

"*Are you fucking kidding me?*" The door to Dr. Merriweather's office, at the top of the stairs, is flung open.

"Willow?" I fumble my pistol back into the holster.

"Were you gonna blast someone with that peashooter?"

"No!" I'm defensive.

"He almost dropped it, did you see?" Josie pulls the lollipop she's sucking on out of her mouth.

"No, I didn't!"

"What are you doing here?" Willow narrows her eyes.

"What are *you* doing here?" I demand. "This is a crime scene."

"Yeah, we're investigating the crime," Josie shoots at me.

"Moron," Willow mutters.

My heart's beating a little fast. Part of me is glad it wasn't actually the murderer up here.

"So, what'd you find?" I ask her.

"Typical man. Shows up, wants to copy a girl's homework."

"Or we can all wait around here while I search the same places you searched, and maybe in that time, the police will stop by and arrest all of us," I say dryly.

"Not Josie. She's special."

I pull out a black light.

"He wasn't murdered here. Why do you need that?" Willow complains as I flick off the lights and close the curtain.

"Oof, it looks like someone was murdered here."

"Seriously?" Willow appears in my phone viewfinder. "That's like semen and pussy-juice stains."

I feel my face get hot when she says the word "pussy."

"Oh, that's—" I drop my phone, bend to pick it up, and realize that I'm practically looking under her skirt. I try not to freak out. "That's, um—"

"Gross! It's gross! We were sitting on that couch. Blech!" Willow makes retching noises.

"I'm going to wash with bleach when I get home." Josie makes a face.

"That explains the panties." Willow sighs then shows me the little plastic baggie containing pink underwear. "Recognize them?"

"What? No!" I hold up my hands.

"They don't belong to Taylor Grace?" She waves them in my face.

"I don't know. I haven't seen her unmentionables."

"Cute. He's cute, isn't he, Willow?" Josie beams. "So, Dr. Merriweather is—er, was—cheating on his wife."

"Motive," Willow and I say at the same time.

"Show him the papers." Josie pokes her friend.

"I'm not—fine." Willow rolls her eyes and thrusts a stack of papers at me.

I whistle. "He was trying to take her for everything."

"Can he do that?"

"He's gonna try. Or was going to, anyway. I don't suppose either of you have a law degree, do you?" I ask.

"I have college loan debt and no usable skills. Sorry." Josie shrugs.

I pull out a little pocket scanner and fold it open.

"Um, what is that? I need that in my life." Willow inspects it.

"One of my college roommate's inventions. I coded the software for it." I preen.

"Well, aren't you clever? Isn't he smart, Willow? Man like that is a good provider." Josie waggles her eyebrows.

I run the documents through the scanner. My phone beeps when they've been uploaded.

"Man," Willow says as she scans through the documents before putting them back into the desk drawer. "Lenore really got lucky Jonah died when he did. She's set up for life."

"She had to have done it, right?"

"We'll see if we can get any clues out of her at the funeral."

The morning of the funeral is even colder and darker than yesterday.

I look longingly at the puffer jacket Nana has hung on the door.

She pokes her head into the room.

"Nana, I'm changing!"

"I used to wipe your bum! And it's still as cute as a button. All that working out—has it paid off yet?" She practically skips around the room.

"Why are you so… happy?"

"It's a great day!"

"Because of the funeral?" I frown.

"Silly goose." She pinches my cheek. "We have Airbnb-ers! They're in town to see the snowy mountains and take in the Christmas market."

"Oh, great. Do you need help getting the carriage house ready?"

"No, bubby. I have a nice couple staying there. This is a big group coming in. So I hope you have a girlfriend because you need to go stay with her for a few days."

I sag.

"Or you can stay with me and Horace. He has a tricked-out RV. The walls are thin, though, so bring headphones!"

"I'll figure something out," I grumble. "And I'll take that down. I have it organized," I tell her as she starts to deconstruct my crime-scene wall. "After the funeral."

"I knew I should have rented an office space," I mumble against my turned-up collar as I head down the sidewalk. I also should have worn my coat.

It might be early to show up at Willow's house to pick her up for the funeral, but I didn't want her and Josie to run off without me.

There's a sign on the front door when I walk up onto the porch and stomp off the snow: *Tinsel & Tea B&B.*

The door flings open.

"Oh, good, there you are," a woman with a Manhattan accent says. "The coffee maker isn't working."

"I told you, it just needs a filter change," a man calls from within the house.

"The coffee machine doesn't have a filter, Artie!"

Several children—the couple's grandkids, probably—race around.

"Now, young man, what time do the carriage rides start, and where exactly are we supposed to go to get one?"

"Agnes, I have a map!" Artie calls.

"Um, in front of the town hall. They should start in an hour or so, I think."

"He thinks?"

The pack of tourists brushes past me. I step into the house.

"Willow!" I call. "Willow?"

I step back outside, unsure what I'm supposed to do about the house.

"Hey there, sonny!"

I bite back a yelp as Beryl pops her head out of the window of a parked car.

"Jeez! The, uh, coffee maker's broken?" I peer at her. "Are you living in your car?"

"Damn right! Got the whole place rented out. I let Willow have the garden shed just in case she wanted some male company to keep her warm at night." She winks at me.

"Is this even legal?"

"Now that Jonah Merriweather's dead, it is. Going to toast his murderer at the funeral!" She cranks the window back up.

I make my way to the backyard, where there's a quaint carriage house. "Willow?" I call up at the window. My voice sounds muffled in the snowy backyard.

There's another B-and-B sign on the front door. That can't be it.

I spin around in the yard. A tiny shed with a slanted roof stands in one corner of the yard, like a potting shed.

"She can't seriously be in here." I stomp through the snow, the white powder muffling my footfalls. "That can't be what her granny means, can it?" I press my face to the foggy square window on the side of the shed and almost choke on my tongue.

Willow's in nothing but a black bra and black panties, her back toward me as she rolls dark tights up her legs.

*Don't look. Don't look.*

But I can't help but stare. She has her hair up off her neck, and she looks—well—I don't think they have scenes like that in film noirs.

I make a strangled noise as she leans forward, turning slightly so I can see the curve of her—

"What the fuck?" Willow screams.

I jump away from the window, trip over my feet, and land in the snow.

The shed door bursts open. Willow's there with a hatchet. She has her tights on but not much else.

"I wasn't looking!" I clap my hands over my eyes. "I swear!"

"Pervert!"

"Don't kill me!"

"Hey!" someone yells from the carriage house. "There are supposed to be quiet hours. And what time is breakfast? I'm going to leave you a bad review."

"Coming right up with that!" Willow chirps.

"Oh my god."

Willow drags me into the shed. It's even smaller on the inside than it looks on the outside. The top of my head almost bangs against the roof. A guinea pig munches on leaves in the corner.

"What the hell? What are you even doing here?"

"I wanted to strategize for the funeral. Can you—" I take off my coat and drape it gingerly over her while she glares at me. "You, uh, that's a, um—" I swallow. "That's a nice funeral outfit."

"That's not what I'm wearing," she snaps, crossing her arms. "Go outside and get those boarders their breakfast while I change."

Willow's boots crunch the ice as she and I walk to the funeral home. I'm carrying a platter of chocolate toffee cupcakes balanced on a warm casserole dish.

"Did you know Lenore well?" I ask.

"No, but you have to bring something to a funeral. We're probably not the only ones using the casserole excuse to attend."

"You weren't lying," I say when we cross the street to the church.

"Gotta love a small-town murder mystery!"

It's bedlam—a sea of people all carrying flowers, cake boxes, and yes, casserole dishes.

"Do you even see Lenore?" Willow asks as we enter the church.

I peer over the crowd. She's there in the back, near the oversized poster of Jonah, surrounded by flowers.

"She doesn't look like a crushed widow," Willow whispers.

"Everyone grieves in different ways, or something like that," I whisper, tugging her over.

Lenore looks like a woman out with her girlfriends, gossiping over a glass of wine, not like someone at a beloved husband's funeral.

"Ohhh, you're the cute PI. This is the one I was telling you about!" Lenore giggles to her friends. "I love a man in a fedora."

"See?" I tell Willow.

"We're so sorry for your loss," Willow says to Mrs. Merriweather.

"Don't be!" She waves a hand. "We don't have his body yet, but we have to do some sort of memorial service. It's a requirement for the life insurance policy. You have to have the obituary, and for that, you have to have the memorial service," Lenore explains to a group of sympathetic women. "Set what you brought on that table over there. My friend's daughter is helping take care of the food."

Willow sets her casserole dish on the groaning table.

"Oh, are those cupcakes?" Bobby, one of the Harrogate PD officers, comes over, his plate piled high with food. "I need to grab one of those before the rest of the town does." He balances a cupcake on his plate.

"Hey, so, Bobby—"

"Hmm? Oh man, this is a good cupcake."

"There's more where that came from," Willow offers. "Did you happen to request the records for Jonah Merriweather's phone yet?"

Bobby is chowing down on the funeral food and asks, "You can do that?"

God help me. "Yeah, you just ask the telecom company," I tell him.

"Oh, well, no." He swallows. "I'll do it after lunch. Oh, did Mrs. Costa make her manicotti?" He plods off.

Lenore lets out a peal of laughter. "I know! He got what was coming to him."

One of her friends tries to shush her.

"I have an alibi. I was watching the Christmas tree lighting, just like everyone else. You should have seen my face when they told me he was dead!"

Her friends all laugh.

"I mean, she couldn't have murdered him, right?" Willow whispers. "If she did, she'd at least try to pretend to be sad. I mean, who murders someone and brags about it?"

"Shockingly, a surprising number of people. They want people to know they got away with it."

Willow frowns and looks at her phone.

"What's wrong?"

"Oh—" She hides her phone from me. "Nothing."

# CHAPTER 11

## Willow

"She's not coming?" I say in disbelief as I stare at the phone and Josie's text message.

"Hey, Willow," Hollis says from my elbow. "I wasn't sure what you and Josie were bringing to the funeral—if it was savory or sweet. I brought some cookies I made with some leftover dough. Hope it's okay. They're sort of like pinwheel Santa's kitchen sink cookies?"

"Josie's not coming," I tell her with a sigh. "Apparently, something came up with her husband and his family."

"Dang, it's the event of the holiday season. Guess I'll have to be your girl Friday." She giggles. "So, who are we investigating? Are we looking for clues?"

"Well." I sigh. "Hughes and I already talked to Lenore."

"Ooh, so there is a man on the horizon. Rose was wondering."

"It's not like that. And since when is Rose observant about anything?"

"Well, we should go talk to Lenore when there's no men around. Then, you know, us women, we like to gossip." Hollis giggles. "Also, she's so deep in the sauce, she'll tell you where all the bodies are buried."

We head back over to the snack table so Hollis can set down the cookies. While she chats about the Jell-O salad Mrs. Rinaldi brought, I notice an elegant woman sifting through the dizzying array of casserole dishes. Something about her is familiar.

The woman's eyes lock with mine for a moment. I glance away so she doesn't think I'm staring. When I look back at the table, the young woman has disappeared.

"There she is." Lenore gestures drunkenly with her wineglass. "Willow made those delicious cupcakes. She's going to be in that baking contest next week, aren't you, dear?"

"I'm so sorry for your loss," Hollis says breathlessly. "Dr. Merriweather was—"

"A dick. A liar and a cheat."

"Oh, you mean like he was having an affair?" Hollis's voice drops.

"I'd bet my life on it," she says. "He always hid his phone and laptop from me. No." She gestures with her wineglass. "I don't care. I'm making bank off this. Make sure, girls, that you take a life insurance policy out on your man as soon"—she snaps her fingers—"as you marry him. The biggest you can get. Because Mama needs to get paid. Thank you, karma!"

"*How could you?*"

The crowd parts.

There is Taylor Grace in a humongous black hat, complete with a veil and a skintight little black dress with a fake fur coat. "You… you witch!" Taylor Grace shrieks.

"Damn." Lilith and her twin sister pull their sunglasses down, affronted.

"He was the only person keeping me sane. Jonah!" Taylor Grace lets out a wail. "Oh, Jonah." She looks like she's getting ready to throw herself over the coffin, except, of course, there is none, so she settles for collapsing on the floor in front of his photo.

Everyone gapes.

Taylor Grace's foot catches the easel, sending something clattering to the floor. A little locomotive. It rolls over to us.

Lenore tries to kick it out of the way, misses, then curses.

"Did Jonah like trains?" I ask, thinking of Gideon.

"Ugh, the trains. I hate them." She drains her wine glass. "The whole house is filled with them. No. Jonah kept them for his father. He had daddy issues. Probably why he became a therapist in the first place."

Her friend refills her glass.

"I told that weirdo in the market he could have them all. Serves my husband right. He kept thinking they were worth money because his father said so. Like I'm going to waste my time trying to sell them when I have this life insurance payout."

"Wait, the weirdo at the market—you mean Gideon?"

"Oh, is that his name?" She sniffs. "Do you know if he does yard work? I want to dig up the stupid Christmas tree my late husband planted in the yard one year. Idiot."

"You need to make more of those Santa's kitchen sink cookies," I tell Hollis. "They were weirdly a big hit at the funeral."

She beams.

I stack the last of the boxes on the dolly to take to the Christmas market stall. I text Josie again to see if she wants to meet me at the stall at some point so I can fill her in on the funeral from yesterday. But as I'm walking to the door, I see a flash of red hair. There's Josie and Lydia with their kids, walking and chatting and laughing. But they don't come into my shop—they just walk right on by. I see Josie pull out her phone, read my text, then put her phone away. I'm crushed.

"She's extremely ADD and forgetful," I remind myself. But still, it stings.

"Yeah, she's got kids now. That's what happens," Hollis says, appearing next to me. "Josie is like those moms who just don't really get along with non-moms. Taylor Grace had that problem with Lydia. Not that I'm judging anyone. I guess we just need to get husbands and babies!" She giggles. "Or you need a new friend circle. Don't worry. I'll be your bestie! I'll be over in a bit with those cookies. Have a post ready to go for the socials."

I plod through the Christmas market, trying to focus on the murder so I don't focus on my imploding friendship. Is Hollis right? Are we growing irreparably apart? Should I just go get knocked up by a Christmas tourist so I have something in my life to be proud of? Then Josie and I could hang out. But she has a rich man supporting her. I would have what? Gran and her illegal Airbnb scheme?

"There you are!" Hughes impatiently grabs the dolly handle from me and practically sprints to my stall. "I have something to show you. Hurry up."

"I have to put these cookies out."

He grabs a pair of gloves and starts stacking cookies, cupcakes, cake pops, and other sweets in the glass cases to entice Christmas market visitors. "So, you know about the Christmas committee and the Christmas cops, right?"

"Yeah, everyone loves a man on horseback. Their legs spread like that... drool."

His face goes red, and I snort.

"Is that payback for me accidentally—*accidentally*"—he holds up a finger—"seeing you change yesterday?"

"You never did apologize," I tease.

"Well, Ms. Price"—his voice lowers to a delicious growl—"I'm ashamed to say, I am very sorry for spying on you. Inadvertently. But what I have here will make it up to you."

"Will it?"

"Okay, so," he says excitedly as he fans out the copies on the counter, "here are all the complaints Jonah Merriweather made to the Christmas committee."

"All of these"—my eyebrows rise—"are his complaints?"

"Yeah, since Thanksgiving."

"There's, like, hundreds."

"Mostly about short-term Airbnb rentals."

"You better not be about to accuse my granny of murder," I warn.

"No way!" He holds up his hands. "Then I'd be implicating my own as well. Stupid Airbnbs. Maybe Jonah was onto something. I still need to find a place to crash tonight."

He sighs. "Anyway—but no. Look here." He pushes three sheets toward me.

"Jonah lodged several complaints against Gideon for trying to sell non-model-train-related items. Looks like Gideon submitted a request to sell cookies?"

"He can't sell cookies. I sell cookies." I shake my head. "No. He'd just go buy some shit from Costco to sell. He doesn't know how to bake."

"In that, you and Dr. Merriweather agree."

"Broken clock," I quip.

"Well, you better file a complaint, then, because Gideon has already"—he shoves more papers at me—"asked for a review of his proposal. He wants to sell Christmas train–themed cookies. And according to the old lady at city hall who slapped my butt, the committee is probably going to approve his request—unless you make a stink or Jonah rises from his snowy grave."

"So this is it." I lean against the stall. "You did it. You solved it."

"Hmm?"

"You solved the murder."

"I mean, it's a pretty good theory," he preens.

"No, like, Gideon killed Jonah. We thought it was because Jonah is perhaps having an affair with Taylor Grace, who Gideon apparently had a thing with, but this is a very clear motive. He had reason to want him dead, profited off his death, and had the means and opportunity to kill him."

"So are we going to the police?"

"No." I grab my phone. "We need a confession first."

"A confession?" Hughes hisses, ducking out of the stall after me. "We can't just go confront a potential murderer."

"I'm not letting the police ruin this investigation. I need my name cleared right now. Gideon!"

He jumps when we enter his stall. It smells even mustier than it did the first time.

"Can I—" He looks up at Hughes, who is tall and menacing behind me in his trench coat, the hat low over his eyes. Gideon gulps. "Help you?" he squeaks.

"I want a confession." I shake the papers at him. "I know what you did. I know what you're doing, and you need to confess to your crimes," I thunder.

"I didn't do anything." Gideon looks like he's going to make a run for it.

Hughes grabs him by the collar and shakes him roughly. "Tell the truth, or we'll drag you down to the precinct right now."

"Okay." Gideon starts sobbing. "Okay, don't hurt me. God. It's probably better that it's all over."

Hughes dumps him onto his stool.

"I can't take the guilt anymore. It's killing me. This whole thing was a mistake."

"So you're saying Jonah's death was an accident?"

Hughes gives me a strange look. "His what? I thought you were here about the model train fraud."

"The what?"

Hughes sags on his stool. "There's no money in model trains. Hasn't been since the mid-'90s at least. Oh sure, you can sell some of the older special-edition models from the '40s to the '60s online, but you don't get anywhere near the money you got when my great-uncle ran this place." He looks around wistfully. "Model train enthusiasts are a dying breed."

"Well, it's good to have a hobby."

"It's not my hobby. I hate model trains," he says vehemently. "All the old people in town think I love them, though, so people are constantly gifting me their model train sets, willing me their model train sets, or dumping the model train sets of their deceased relatives on me. Sure, people like to look at the Christmas sets in the winter, but no one wants to pay to see them. The city throws me a few bones every winter to set up model train sets in the city hall, and some businesses want them for the winter, but it doesn't pay the stall fees or my shop fees." Gideon looks dejected. "Jonah thought he could do a better job at it than I could. He thought I was purposefully not selling the trains so I could make money on the internet. But that's not how it works!"

"So what's the fraud?" Hughes asks, confused.

Gideon sighs and pulls out his phone. He pauses then gives in and shoves the phone at Hughes. "This is how I make money."

On the screen is a slow-motion video of a miniature train in a miniature town. Then, suddenly, the train blows up. There's a soundtrack of screaming.

"Oh my god." Hughes laughs. "You make these videos? I've seen these all over the internet. I love these videos. They're crazy!"

"Yes. I blow up model trains for money." Gideon starts crying.

"And Jonah found out, so you killed him?" I'm still hopeful we can solve this mystery.

"God, no. I have enough money saved up and enough trains in storage to stop maintaining this stall. It's just the guilt..."

"But the missing train from his office—"

"He doesn't keep trains in his office," Gideon says impatiently. "They're all at his house. His wife is dumping them all on me. It's guilt, you see. People's parents, grandparents, uncles loved their trains, and they want to think that they're going to a good home. Jonah found my videos. He recognized one of the sets. Apparently, his dad made it and gave it to a friend. That video did get me a small bourbon sponsorship, though." He sits back down. "I can't keep living the lie."

"Oh, but everyone loves the Christmas train sets."

"Yeah, yeah, it's the small-town charm. Do you know how demoralizing it is to have people stop at your shop, take a photo, then leave? I can't afford to hire anyone, so I just have to sit here." He kicks a shelf.

"Well, it seems like you knew Jonah fairly well," I finally segue awkwardly. "Do you know who killed him?"

Gideon shrugs.

"Do you know who he might have been having an affair with?"

"Like, all of his female patients."

"All of…"

Hughes and I look at each other.

"So we could have a whole other list of suspects."

# CHAPTER 12
# Hughes

"We need a list of all his patients," I tell Willow. "Did you see one in his office? Or, like, a schedule book or anything?"

Willow shakes her head. "The police must have taken it."

"It's probably on his phone, which is missing."

"Jonah seems a little too old-school for that," Willow counters. "He seems like he writes things down with a fountain pen."

We flip through the photos I took of the office just to verify we didn't miss the appointment book.

"Did you see patient files or anything?"

"They could be at his house."

"Or at the police station."

Winston Girthman pats his belly when we walk in.

"Did you make more of that tater tot hot chicken casserole, Willow?" he asks hopefully.

"No, but I can if you do us a favor," she coaxes.

"Oh. I hope it's not the medical examiner's report."

"We were looking for patient files, but there's a report?"

"Well, we got the medical examiner to look at the body after he got back from his cruise, and he thinks it wasn't electrocution, but he's not sure. They will send it to the county, however."

"So not an electrocution."

"Could still be a hanging." Winston beams. "Suck it, fire department!" He shakes his fist.

"Speaking of the cause of death… we wanted to see if you all logged an appointment book into evidence," I say.

"I really shouldn't be giving it to you." Winston squirms.

"I'll give you cookies at my shop for life," Willow sings.

"For life?"

"*The shop's got five months tops, so good luck,*" Willow mutters so only I can hear, though I'm not sure if she means it. "Sure! For life. A cookie a day." Willow forces a smile.

"Or a cupcake?" Winston asks hopefully.

"Or a cupcake a day," Willow amends.

"You're still going to make those chocolate toffee ones, right?" Winston asks anxiously.

"I'll bring you a whole box if you bring me that appointment book," she promises.

"Shh, not so loud. Well, I'm happy to talk to you about your grandmother's memory issues. Just right this way to my office—okay?" He leads us into a messy room packed with stuff.

"So, this is everything we took from Dr. Merriweather's office," he says.

Willow and I dig through the box.

There's not much in there—a plastic plant, an old clock that doesn't work, a book on Jung.

"Why did you take these things as evidence?" I look at Winston.

"We had to fill up the box."

"Great." I pull out the appointment book. "At least there's that."

Willow and I each start at one end of the appointment book, quickly photographing the pages with the lists of names. I barely register them. Her head is almost touching mine. Her hair tickles my cheek every time she turns a page, our fingers brushing as we hurry to collect the evidence, trying to photograph as many pages as we can before Winston tells us we have to go.

"Oh, shoot, the chief's back from vacation early." Winston jumps up. "You have to go."

I grimace when we step back into the cold.

"I didn't get all of the pages." Willow adjusts her scarf.

"We have a pretty good list, though."

We scroll through the photos as we stroll through the Christmas market.

"Well, here's Taylor Grace, obviously. There's Donna Reeves—she runs one of the ornament stalls, I think."

"It would be helpful to know how he actually died," I muse.

"Hanging, you think?"

"If it's hanging, Lenore couldn't have done it, right?"

"Unless she had a helper."

"Dr. Merriweather could have multiple affair partners."

"She could have convinced someone to do it." Willow blows out a breath and wraps her arms around herself.

"Hey, do you want to go grab—I was going to say coffee, but you're probably tired of it. Maybe pizza and a beer, and we can look at our potential evidence?"

"Oh. I can't."

For some reason, I feel disappointed. Why? It's not like I was asking her out. Or was I? That can't be right.

"I have to go help Gran with the prep for the ugly-sweater party tomorrow," she explains. "You're coming, right?"

"I think I'd be drawn and quartered if I didn't. I hear it's the event of the holiday season."

She reaches up to pat my chest then tug at the lapels of the too-thin trench coat. "Well, stay warm."

"You don't think…" I trail off.

"What?"

"Ah, never mind."

"What?" she insists.

"Uh, just need to figure out where I'm going to live tonight."

"You need to go to Costco and buy a garden shed."

"Guess there's not room enough for two?" I joke.

"Unless you really want to get cozy."

Part of me wants to say I do.

"If you want—and I can't believe I'm saying this—you can crash in my shop. If you want."

"Really?"

"But you should bring a warm blanket. The ovens will come on at 3 a.m., but still."

I don't want to tell her what I was about to ask: Do you think our grandmothers could have had something to do with Dr. Merriweather's murder after all?

# CHAPTER 13

# *Willow*

"Are all the drunk people really going to appreciate these garlands?" I complain to myself as I haul the sled full of evergreen boughs through the Christmas market. Maybe I should have taken Hughes up on his offer for a date. *Not a date*. Just beer and pizza. "You can't let a man buy you food then insist he perform manual labor for your granny."

Breathing hard, I adjust the pull on the sleigh and make sure I'm not about to lose any garlands. I need to lay off the cookies. Though, speaking of cookies, a gingerbread latte would be really good right now. A girl needs caffeine if she's going to perform unpaid labor for her grandmother.

The Jingle Bites Café is bustling.

It's a small town, and I'm not the only one with a sleigh, carriage, or dog stroller of packages from the Christmas market parked outside.

"Oh!" Rose exclaims when she sees me. "Did you come to get Hollis's bag? She left it here."

"Oh, uh, no, but I'll take it to her," I promise Rose before she can protest.

I bus a few tables then grab a tray and extra napkins and take them out into the café, wondering if it would be super un-feminist of me to try wheedling Hughes into lugging all my garlands home to Gran.

Weird… there's that tall, svelte woman with the glossy hair again. Where do I know her from…?

"Oof! Sorry, Mrs. Levensworth!" I apologize as I drop Hollis's bag, my phone, and the napkins all over the floor. "Shoot, shoot, shoot." I scoop everything up to dump Hollis's stuff back into her tote.

Then stare.

There, at the bottom of the bag, is a tiny toy train.

"What the what?" I take it out.

It's a model train like Gideon sells in his shop, still in its little plastic box.

No freaking… no way. Is Hollis the murderer?

I dump the napkins on the nearest table and hurry outside.

"Oh, hey, Willow."

"Hughes, oh my gosh."

He gives me an odd look and adjusts the duffel bag over his shoulder. "Gran made me clear out my murder clues. I thought I could stash them here. If that's still okay…"

"Here, with Hollis?" I squawk. "Um, actually—"

"Oh, I mean, it's okay if I can't stay here." He shuffles his feet.

"Uh, no, I'm not leaving anyone out in the cold." I laugh nervously, looking over my shoulder. "But actually, I think you're just going to bunk with me and Gran tonight. Yep. That's the plan."

"Aren't you busy? I know you were party planning." He gives me a quizzical look.

"Yes, I have a thousand pounds of garland here." I gesture wildly. "We need to talk."

"About the case? Did you find another clue?"

"Not here," I hiss and pull him to the side entrance of the shop and into the kitchen.

We're enveloped by the heat and the smell of cookies. I immediately start sweating.

Hughes unbuttons the trench coat. "So, what d'ya got? Crack the case wide open?"

I drool at him. He gives me a questioning look as he peels off that stupid trench coat to reveal a stupidly hot body. What kind of man has a body like that and hides it under a trench coat?

"I, um—" I'm going to pass out. "Well, there's been a development," I squawk.

"You don't look so good. What happened?" He grabs my face. "Willow, what is it?"

"*I want to have sex with you.*" Actually, no, that's not what I say. "Just, gosh, it's warm in here." I shove Hollis's bag at him, drag off my coat, and fan myself. Yeah, I really need to start working out or something. This is ridiculous. "I think—okay, this is going to sound crazy, but I think Hollis is the murderer."

He huffs out a laugh. "Hollis? She's so friendly, and she likes to bake. Isn't she your right-hand man?"

"Means, motive, opportunity." I tick off the items on my fingers.

"Motive?"

I pull the little train out of her bag. "I'm 100 percent—okay, maybe 90 percent—sure she took this from Dr. Merriweather's office." I show him the photos I've taken of the blank space on the shelf. "It's a souvenir or a reminder or something of Dr. Merriweather. And she goes back and forth to my stall all day. She could have rigged something to murder Jonah."

"So, we know she was a patient? And if so, what would he have done to make her murder him?"

I shrug. "Cheating on her with Taylor Grace?"

"We actually don't know that they were sleeping together," Hughes argues.

"You're so naïve."

He pulls out his phone.

"Are you calling the police?"

"I'm checking the log of names... Hmm," he says. "I don't see a Hollis."

"Darn."

Frowning, he looks harder at the list of names we got from the therapist. "Is Hollis her actual name?"

"Uh, no. It's Katie Hollister. There were a lot of Katies in class that year—"

"Here it is. Katherine Hollister. Damn, Willow. I think you just found us another suspect."

"Shit, maybe those are her underwear. I need to—" I look back toward the Christmas market and my stall, where Hollis is currently. "It's all circumstantial. I need more clues."

My phone rings.

"Gran... yes, we're coming—*Hughes, let's walk and talk*," I tell him, gesturing.

"Oh, you're with a man? Never mind." Gran cackles on the other end of the line. "That Airbnb-er was complaining to me that you're running some sort of cathouse out of the shed."

I clap a hand to my face while a smirk plays around Hughes's mouth.

"No, that's not what's going on here."

"Good. Now, you know I'm on Team Willow, but real talk: You're not in your twenties anymore. You can't be making a man like Hughes pay to have sex with you. Now, a man like Trudy's son? Yeah, go ahead and make him pay. Make him shower too."

"Okay, thanks for the advice. I'll definitely incorporate that into my day-to-day life. Gotta go. See you in a bit."

Hughes has a sly grin on his face. "You look cute in that sweater." His hands circle my waist. "I'd definitely pay big bucks to have sex with you."

*I'm not going to think about him spying on me,* I tell myself firmly. *It's not hot. It's embarrassing.* "Say, do you want to—" I grab his bicep. It's as hard as a rock under the black turtleneck. "Do you want to use those big, strong man muscles"—*Willow, what actual the fuck?*—"to haul some garlands?"

"Yeah," he says, his lip catching in his teeth. "Yeah? On one condition. You let me take you out on our pizza-and-beer date."

"Okay," I squawk. "It's a date."

# CHAPTER 14

# Hughes

A date! I have a date. Shit, I have a date. I need to plan something, figure out topics of conversation, pick a pizza place. "You're not gluten-free, are you?"

"Ooh," she makes a face. "I respect all dietary choices, but bread and cheese are my two major food groups, and I cannot have—"

"Don't worry, our future children will come out of the womb eating pizza rolls."

Did I seriously just talk about impregnating her? She's going to think I'm a pervert. Though with the way that sweater hugs her curves, she wouldn't be far off.

"Well, I can't wait for you to give me that baby, then," she jokes.

As I pick up the entire sleigh and set it on the front porch, Willow's eyes widen.

"You want it here, right? Or I can take it around back."

"No, here is good. I have to put them on the mantel and around the stairs."

"Okay, cool. I can come over later to help you," I offer.

"Oh, are you off?"

"I, um—" I clear my throat. "If you must know, I am going to go get a warmer coat."

Nana is humming in the kitchen and baking when I step in and shake the snow off my collar.

"I saw you moved your things out." She kisses me noisily on the cheek. "Good boy. We're officially booked up for the rest of the Christmas season! I'm going to do a Galentine's special in February. Oh, this is a merry Christmas!" She adds peppermint bits into the batter.

"You making a cake for the ugly-sweater party?" I sample the batter.

"Oh, this is just for our Airbnb guests. It's the breakfast part of the B-and-B. I'm making a bonfire spiced Bundt." She pulls out a Ken doll. "Doesn't that look like Jonah? We'll douse it with bourbon and light it on fire at midnight!"

"Nana..."

She beams at me.

For a minute, all I can think about are those citations that Jonah made against my nana. She's an old lady, I tell myself. There's no way that she's murdered a middle-aged man. That's not even physically possible, right?

"Nana, I don't think that we should be celebrating Jonah's death. People might think one of us killed him. I'm trying to investigate his murder."

"Oh, shoot." Nana licks her finger. "I dropped the spoon." She grabs the stove and starts to drag it.

"I'll get it."

Nana shoos me away. "I've been lifting weights down at the community center."

The stove scrapes as Nana pulls it away from the wall. I grimace. Maybe she could have killed Jonah. She's strong enough.

"I just think"—I gently take the Ken doll—"that it would be a little disrespectful, considering Jonah just passed away. His family is still grieving."

"Who, Lenore?" She snorts. "She won't give a shit."

"Yeah, I heard Lenore had a lot to gain by his death," I say lightly, wondering if Nana will give me the small-town senior gossip.

"A lot to gain? That's underselling it."

"Yeah, that life insurance policy was like a million dollars."

"Oh." Nana laughs as she scrapes the bowl. "That's nothing. She's lucky he was too busy trying to ruin people's livelihoods to run off with another woman and divorce her. She inherited tens of millions from her childless aunt, plus a number of properties around town that the Svenssons are highly interested in purchasing. I bet she never marries again. Can't have a man after your assets. Present company notwithstanding. I know you won't run off with a woman's hard-earned money. You have your own, don't you, dear?" She pats my arm. "Don't worry about Jonah. No one liked him. Now, are you staying at a sweetheart's house for the winter holidays?"

I think of Willow. Was she just joking? Does she really want me to stay with her? Was it flirting? I wish I'd just kissed her in the bakery, let my hands drift over her curves. "Uh—"

"You need to get on it," Nana tuts. "There's a new girl back in town—Mrs. Locke's granddaughter. She's a nice girl. Very pretty. Went to California and really toned up. I'd kill for that behind." She laughs to herself. "Kill."

It makes my stomach flip-flop. "Where's my coat?"

"Your trench?" She wipes her hand on a towel.

"My red one."

"Oh, wonderful. You'll look so handsome in that. I even embroidered some snowflakes on it. I wanted it to be more festive and fun for you. And I was just at old Mrs. Banner's house—she made you a matching hat and mittens."

"Great. Sounds warm. I'm heading over to Willow's."

"Take the ham over there. It's in the garage fridge."

I relax as I step out into the cold and flex my arms in the coat. It's nice to be warm, though I do look dumb in this puffy jacket. There's even a little Rudolph at the edge. I look like I'm one of the Christmas market cops.

"Hughes!"

Fuck. I stand stock-still, but of course, Taylor Grace sees me in the bright-red coat.

"I need you to know that I'm feeling very stressed." She lays into me, saying, "I need to know what's going on with the investigation."

"Well, we're working on it."

"*We?* We who?" Taylor Grace pounces on the word.

"I mean *I* am working on it," I backtrack.

"What is this?" She thumbs the jacket. "What are you wearing?"

*Jesus.*

"Just a warmer coat."

"But why? Why are you wearing it?"

"It's cold."

"Yes, but why are you wearing this coat?"

"Why wouldn't I?"

"Why are you dodging the question?"

"I'm not. I just answered."

Talking to her is disorienting—like being trapped in a riptide.

"It's Willow, isn't it? She told you to wear this, didn't she? Did she do this embroidery?" The tears fill her eyes. "You don't understand what I'm going through right now. I need a strong man, a leader in my life."

I start trying to edge around her. It's hard with the oversized pan of ham.

"You're gaslighting me. This is what Jonah warned me about." Her eyes are wide and crazy.

"He warned you about me?"

"He was jealous." She raises a fluttering hand to her forehead. "He could tell that I'm so deeply in love with you. I think—I think—" She leans up to me. "I think we're soulmates."

I stand frozen solid, even with the warm jacket, as she grabs my shoulder and my jaw and kisses me noisily, moaning.

"Um," I stammer. "I really do think that's—*oh, shit.*"

Willow stands at the end of my grandmother's walkway and stares me down. She looks hurt. "I just had to drop this off."

"Willow—"

She doesn't respond, just dumps the bag and flees.

# CHAPTER 15

## Willow

Oh. My. God. Why did I think he was attracted to me?

I pace around the stall. Call Josie again. No answer. Crap.

I'm so stupid. Of course a guy like him wants Taylor Grace. Sex with crazy girls is amazing, right? A guy with a body like that and a huge bank account—he doesn't want to deal with a girl who lives at her grandmother's house, has no savings, and has a certifiably insane ex-best friend.

Though the crazy part certainly doesn't seem to dissuade him.

"Ugh, I can't believe I tried to invite him over to basically live with me. That's so thirsty. He must have thought I was such a weirdo. I misread signals—that's what I always do. I misread signals. I miss red flags."

"Willow, there you are."

I flinch.

"I'm sorry, did I startle you?" Taylor Grace smiles. "Oh, Willow," she says with fake friendliness. "I just wanted to check in, see how you were doing. I feel like all this"—she waves her arm—"business stuff has really come between our friendship. And I just want you to know"—she grabs my arm—"that I really value your friendship. Why don't we go get dinner later? Just us girls. Get drinks and apps. We can gossip about guys. I have to tell you about Hughes," she drawls. "I cannot wait for my divorce to be finalized."

Ah, there it is. She knows he rejected me, and she wants to gloat. It's crappy because part of me still wants to go hang out with her. When Taylor Grace is on, she's funny and smart. But it's hiding a cesspit of crazy.

"I have to run this shop."

"Right, right," she says sympathetically. "I forgot, you do need the money, don't you?"

I have whiplash. My head hurts from grinding my teeth.

"And you need the distraction. I see Josie's gone back to her old ways."

"What?"

"I think she just really doesn't want to be your friend anymore. I mean, she and Lydia are spending so much time together. I was talking to Hollis about it earlier. She agrees with me. She's worried Josie is being really callous with your feelings." Taylor Grace nods sagely.

Hollis and Taylor Grace… They've been in cahoots this whole time. The realization is sudden, clear. They both teamed up to kill Jonah, probably out of jealousy. Taylor Grace is crazy, and maybe Hollis is too. I don't know.

"I saw her and Lydia out with their children. She has such a cute little baby. Did you ever want to get married and have children?" Taylor Grace says in that syrupy, passive-aggressive way.

"I—I don't know anymore."

"Probably for the best. All Lydia talks about are those stupid children. They're terrible too. So dirty. But everyone is all, 'Oh, poor Lydia with her three children, one on the way. What can we do to make Lydia's life easier?' Why don't my parents ever do anything for me? No one does anything for me."

*Like put myself in debt to make* your *dreams of a Christmas café a reality? Like that?* I want to scream.

Taylor narrows her eyes. "You know what Lydia said to me at family dinner? It's so crazy. You're going to die when you hear this." She grabs my arm like we're still friends or something. "She told me that Hollis is her *best friend*. Lydia is *my* sister. That makes her my best friend. Me. Not Hollis. Hollis is just sucking up to my sister because that's how everyone treats Lydia. She can do no wrong. She's perfect. She's a mom. Hollis is probably getting ready to wear her skin as a suit."

"Taylor Grace, I'm—" I straighten. "I really need to go. I have to work the shop, so unless you want to help—"

"Help you?" The fury is back. "Help you? This is my shop. You need to help me!" she screams. "I do literally everything around here. Everything!" Taylor Grace storms out.

My ears are still ringing when, a few minutes later, Hollis creeps in.

"Sorry, I was hiding out in the yarn stall. I just can't face her right now."

We stare in the direction in which Taylor Grace stormed off.

"I really think she's gotten more unhinged in the past couple of months." Hollis sounds a little shell-shocked.

"Yeah, I noticed that too," I say dryly then remember who I'm talking to. Right. Hollis is potentially a murderer. Back on track. "What do you think triggered it?" I ask her carefully.

"Oh, Willow." She grabs my hand. "I don't think it was you. Taylor Grace is just like that with people. She's all besties with them, then the discard happens. It's like that with everyone. I tried to be her friend—really, I did—but she's just so… Taylor. I want to be there for her, I do, but—" She sighs. "And her birthday is coming up next month. She keeps saying she wants to go on a big girls' trip, but, like, who's going to plan it? Lydia? Now she's saying that she has something bigger and better planned and her fake friends aren't invited."

"She's probably planning a romantic getaway." I think of Hughes.

Hollis grimaces. "She told you about the affair, then."

"Oh, yeah," I say, trying to lead her on. Is this the confession?

"I seriously—I did everything for her, you know." Hollis is anguished.

*Including killing for her?*

"I really tried to be her friend. I lent her my car, let her live with me, spent hours on the phone with her each night. She did nothing but complain about everyone in my life, trying to alienate me from my friends and family. From you, from my mom, from Lydia. From—" She chewed on her lip. "I just made horrible decisions when I was with her."

"That's understandable, Hollis." I try to sound reassuring. "You couldn't have known."

"It's like she sucks you into a trap."

"Exactly. The same thing happened to me, then I found myself in horrible debt with this shop in the red. All this money spent for nothing. It almost makes me want to kill something. I get so angry and frustrated sometimes."

"I know." Hollis sobs. "She just ruins your life, and then, when you try to explain it to someone, they just think you're crazy. And then you find yourself doing horrible things, and you think, 'Oh my gosh, I *am* crazy.'"

"I completely understand." I decide to make my move. "What happened exactly with Jonah?"

"Oh, you... you know." She collapses, wailing. "Oh, Jonah. It was a mistake. I didn't mean for it to happen."

"Just tell me how he died."

"How he—" Her eyes widen. She blinks up at me. "I don't know how he died. I thought you were talking about the affair."

"The affair?"

She sniffles. "Jonah and I were sleeping together."

"But you said you did something horrible."

"I did," she wails. "The reason I'm working for you? Taylor convinced me you were evil, that you were out to get her. I believed her lies. She claimed she had an abusive childhood and that everyone always lied to her, and she was convinced that you were trying to steal her company. She wanted me to spy on you."

I wish she would take this company. I would love to just be rid of it.

"I know," Hollis says earnestly. "You're such a hard worker, and you always make sure Rose and I get paid, and you give people free food. I saw that I was wrong. I'm so sorry. She and I used to talk so much shit about you." Her chin wobbles. "And I feel so terrible. I hope you can forgive me. I want us to be friends."

I rub her back as she sobs.

"I don't suppose—" I start to ask when she calms down.

"You cannot tell Taylor Grace. Promise?" Hollis begs. "She will go bananas if she finds out that Jonah was having an affair with me. She's so unhinged. Jonah wanted to leave her. He told me. He said, at first, he thought she was just a poor, abused girl, then he talked to her sister."

"He talked to Lydia?"

Hollis nods. "Lydia told him that Taylor Grace had a charmed childhood and was never abused, that she's always been insane. And that she's dangerous."

"Jonah told me that he tried to bring it up in a therapy session, and Taylor Grace went ballistic. He told her that they needed some distance, then—"

"Shit. I knew it. Taylor Grace killed Jonah." I pace in front of the counter.

"That's what I think," Hollis whispers. "You should come hang out with me and Lydia. Lydia cannot stand Taylor Grace. She and I really bonded over her craziness."

"Yeah, Taylor Grace was complaining about it to me."

"I'm not surprised. She is very possessive about her sister." Hollis's eyes widen. "You need to tell your friend Josie to be careful. Taylor Grace will probably go after her next."

# CHAPTER 16
# Hughes

"Good, you brought the ham. Now you need to slice that up into small pieces. Watch the rolls while you're in here," Willow's grandmother tells me when I stomp the snow off my boots at the back door to her house.

"I gotta go clean the bedrooms. The tourists checked out late today, even though they knew I have the party. Willow was supposed to do it. Have you seen her? Where'd she run off to? You didn't pass her coming from your granny's house?" Beryl asks.

"Um, I'm not sure," I lie, still reeling from the kiss and from Willow's reaction.

Dammit, Taylor Grace. Did she ruin what I had with Willow? And what did I have exactly? I'm pretty sure she likes me—or liked me prior to Taylor Grace kissing me, anyway. Jeez. How did I blow that?

Then I wonder: Did Taylor Grace know Willow was there? Did she kiss me just to make her mad? My sister always liked to say girls were way meaner than boys.

Now I sound like Taylor Grace. Paranoid and crazy. But if she does get that crazy jealous, then maybe Willow's right. Taylor could have killed Dr. Merriweather out of jealousy.

While I hate to think that I had a murderer right under my nose as a client—I mean, what kind of private eye would I even be?—it's better than my nana being the murderer. And she's not making it any easier to think otherwise.

The back door slams open, then there's Willow, smacking containers of cupcakes down on the counter. Her mouth is a flat line. "You can go. You don't have to be here."

"I'm helping with the party," I remind her, setting down the knife.

"We don't need your help."

"Look, we have to talk."

"There's nothing to talk about." Her voice has an edge. She shoves past me to wash off pomegranates in the sink.

I grab her arm and push her against the counter, feeling her struggle against me. "Look, Willow. I didn't kiss Taylor Grace."

"Are you kidding me, you stupid, lying—"

I grab her other wrist before she can slap me. She glares up at me, fuming.

"I don't know why I even care. I hope you two are miserable together and she ruins your life and kills you like she did Jonah," Willow spits.

"Well, damn."

"And don't say I'm bad-mouthing your 'client'"—she makes air quotes—"either, because I have evidence from Hollis."

I let her jerk out of my grasp.

"Taylor Grace was having an affair with Jonah, and he was going to break up with her," Willow says in a rush. "I just don't know how she strung up the body, but she was at the Christmas tree lighting ceremony, so she definitely had the opportunity."

I pull out my phone from my pants pocket and thumb through Taylor's messages.

Willow's face goes scarlet when she sees the photos.

"This is what you two are texting about?"

"She barely knew me, and she sent me these photos like thirty minutes after our first meeting. In hindsight, it might have been a red flag. Point is"—I tap on the weights—"she is capable of dragging a body. Jonah doesn't work out. He's not that heavy."

"Glad you're getting your jollies while working. What a way to multitask. No wonder you like being a PI." She tries to wiggle out from under me, but I keep her pinned against the cabinets with my hip.

"She can, and—don't try and run away, I need you to hear this. We're working on a case. Focus—Taylor Grace kissed me. I didn't kiss her, and I couldn't very well drop the ham to push her off, could I? Nana would kill me. But no argument from me—I think Taylor's crazy, and I hope she did kill Jonah because otherwise…" I lick my lip and lean down to whisper to her.

She makes a strangled noise.

"I think our grandmothers could maybe, possibly, be guilty as well. Maybe."

"That's not—"

I clap a hand to her mouth. "Shh!"

"Our grandmothers couldn't have killed him. It has to have been Taylor Grace." Her voice drops at the end. "We will never speak of their potential involvement again. Besides, I live here, and apparently, you're about to move in here too."

"Really? So you forgive me for the kiss?" I murmur.

"The assault."

"She's just jealous of you." I smirk down at Willow, trace the curl of hair that has escaped from the messy bun. "Taylor knows I don't want to kiss her."

Willow swallows, staring unblinking up at me. "You don't?"

"Nah."

"Well, that's probably a good thing because she gets really upset when you don't call her by her full name." Willow licks her lips.

"Yeah, I noticed." I lean in.

Before I can capture her mouth, there's whispering and giggling from the doorway.

Willow jumps, banging her forehead into my chin.

"What the—"

Willow follows me as I peer around the corner to see our two elderly grandmothers holding onto each other and grinning like mad.

"Oh, we didn't mean to interrupt." Beryl and Nana give each other knowing looks. "Go back to what you're doing."

"He was about to kiss her," Nana crows.

Willow keeps clearing her throat behind me, fussing with her clothes. "I guess we'd better get working on this party." She looks a little frazzled.

My chest feels too cold now that she's no longer pressed against me.

"What a wonderful Christmas surprise! Willow's not going to be a virgin anymore." Beryl claps her hands.

"You're a virgin?" I yelp.

"What? No! You are." She points accusingly.

"No, he's not. You take that back," Nana says, jumping to my defense. "You're not, are you?" she whispers out of the side of her mouth.

"No. I know how this all works." I gesture awkwardly.

"Wonderful! I'm going to cancel the Airbnb guest I have coming to the carriage house and let you two have an early Christmas—not the big house," Nana warns me. "I finally got that rented out. And to think it was a murder that made true love happen." Nana swoons. "Jonah being murdered is the best thing to ever happen to us!"

# CHAPTER 17

## Willow

I'm so close to nailing Taylor Grace. She murdered Jonah and tried to blame it on me, and now she's trying to steal my man.

Wait, my man?

I look across the room to where Hughes is talking to some of our grandmothers' friends. Now that he's ditched the trench coat and the fedora—and I'm on my second cup of too-strong Christmas punch—I could be convinced to admit that he is pretty hot, and I could see myself—with a few more cups of punch—sleeping with him.

Tonight.

Maybe.

But probably.

We're only half an hour in, but the party's hopping.

The crowd titters when a tall blond man enters the room and looks around as he takes off his coat.

Mace, Josie's husband, maneuvers through the space. "I thought Josie was here," he says, frowning. He sounds concerned.

"Oh! No, she said she went back home to get changed," I tell him. "I haven't seen her at all this afternoon."

"You're sure she's not here? There's no answer when I call her."

I can feel Mace getting more distressed by the second.

"We'll find her. She probably got distracted by something. You know how she is." I give him a pained smile.

He doesn't return it.

"I'm sure she's fine."

"There's a murderer running loose around town." Mace's voice is dangerously flat. "I'm going to call the police, and—"

"Oh, Josie!" Gran cries, running to the door, where another pack of guests is arriving. "Isn't that the cutest sweater? Did you see her sweater?"

Mace's shoulders drop in relief. "Josie, where were you?"

"I got a hole in my sweater, and I had to buy some yarn to fix it, then I realized, duh, I actually don't know how to knit, so I went to the Christmas market to find a new sweater, and I just lost track of time," my friend rambles.

"You're such a disaster," Mace says affectionately.

"Ooh, are those cupcakes?" Josie perks up.

"The ones in the back have extra gummy snowmen. Help yourself. Be back in a sec," I tell her, still feeling a little shaky.

Like anyone's going to murder Josie. She's Mace Svensson's wife. No murderer is that stupid. I'm just being drunk and paranoid. I grab the bundle of coats from the couch, ferry them to one of the upstairs bedrooms, and dump them onto the bed.

"I need to put the Brie-and-prosciutto pinwheels in the oven," I tell myself as I mentally go through the to-do list. They're going fast. And I stare down at my hands—they're covered in blood.

Oh God. I look around, turning my hands this way and that in the lamplight. I flick on the overhead light. Am I bleeding? Did I get stabbed? I didn't have blood on my hands earlier, right?

I blink, hoping it's the punch and I'm drunk, but no—blood. Not from me.

I tear through the coats on the bed. Then I find it. I can't tell if it's a man's or a woman's coat. It's black, and it's covered in blood. The murderer. It has to be the murderer's. They're here at the party, and they've killed again. With that much blood, it has to be on *someone's* clothes, right? I just need to survey the guests—the hundreds of guests who are in Gran's large Victorian house, spilling out into the front yard, on the back deck, out in the back yard with the firepit.

I stand on the back deck, looking out over the crowd in the dim light. Oh, and everyone is wearing some shade of red, so yeah, it's going to be really easy to see blood smears. I chug my punch. But I have to find the murderer.

"It's her," Hollis whispers to me.

I jump out of my skin. "Her who?"

Hollis looks at me like I'm crazy. "The author of all her pain. The traitor herself."

"What?"

"Maris." Hollis nods her chin to the elegant woman—the same one I saw at the funeral.

"Wait, that's Maris? Taylor Grace made her sound like a troll." I stare at her. She's talking to Hughes's granny. "She doesn't seem crazy."

"I know, right?" Hollis whispers.

"I want to go talk to her. But—" I chew my lip.

"Yeah, I know."

"Taylor Grace would freak out."

"She always said that Maris screwed her out of her business."

Hollis and I stare.

"I felt so sorry for Taylor Grace," I admit. "That's why I covered for her so much on the Jingle Bites Café, because I didn't want her to think I was screwing her over like Maris."

"It really makes you question her whole narrative, doesn't it? It's just lies on lies on lies with Taylor Grace." Hollis shakes her head. "She bad-mouthed Maris to everyone, made herself out as a victim."

"Now she's doing it to me," I say bitterly. "I hate that I fell for it."

"We all fell for it."

"Oh my god, hey, girls!" Josie grabs me in a hug then hugs Hollis. "Lydia's here somewhere," she tells Hollis. "She was asking about you, and I was like, 'I'm sure Hollis is here. She and Willow are such good friends.'"

"Oh, I have a present for her. I was going to give her…" Hollis heads off into the crowd.

"Sorry I'm late," Josie says breathlessly.

"I heard the saga."

"I've been so scatterbrained lately. For a second, I thought I was preggo, then nope. I feel like I've been bailing on you."

"Mace was more concerned."

She wrinkles her nose. "He thinks I'm about to get murdered."

"We haven't caught the murderer yet, so he's right to be worried," I remind her.

"We?" Josie asks pointedly.

"Er, the police?"

"Or do you mean you and Hughes?" Josie licks her lips.

My face reddens. "We're not—that's not—"

"Ida said she saw you two canoodling in the Christmas market."

"We weren't canoodling. We were looking for clues. I'm trying to solve the case," I protest.

"Are you close?"

"Yeah." I whisper all the clues about Taylor Grace to her as Josie helps me put out more Christmas-themed snacks.

"Damn. I mean, you did think it was her from day one," Josie remarks as she shoves another tray of reindeer nibbles and stocking-stuffing muffins into the oven.

"Yeah, I'm trying to remain impartial, though. I mean, I can't pin a murder on her just because I'm jealous of her kissing Hughes."

Josie grabs me. "She what?"

I can't stop grinning at her.

"Why are you smiling? She tried to steal your man. Well, the man I've picked for you."

"He says he likes me." I finally let it out. "I wanted to tell you, but there was no time. I think he almost kissed me in the kitchen today. He was pressed right up against me. I really must be sex starved because it was the most action I've gotten in a while," I admit.

"It's all the threats of violence that are making you horny. Don't let him do the nasty in the garden shed. Make him spring for a hotel."

"You can't get a hotel during Christmastime. Besides, all the B-and-B owners gossip, and the whole town will hear about it."

"So stake your claim."

"He's a catch."

"Ooh, girl gossip!" Gran throws her arms around us. "Doris already said that you and Hughes could do your wedding at the Broughton Estate, where she works. She says she's got an in. But I think you should get married in the gazebo."

"Everyone gets married in the gazebo," Josie complains.

"We haven't even kissed yet. We can't get married, Gran."

"You need to get on that. I'm not getting any younger. You want more than one kid, don't you?" Gran swats my hip. "I'll be dead and in the ground if you keep waiting. You need to lock Hughes down before someone else does." Gran throws the freezer open. "Shoot, are we really out of the maple bacon twists?"

"I made a ton of them, remember, Josie? We made all those a few days ago at the Jingle Bites?"

"IIII—" Josie makes a face. "Forgot to get those from the shop. That's actually what I went to do, then the sweater thing happened. I'll go get them now."

"No, Mace will kill me if you wander off again. I'll get them. BRB." I grab my keys.

Gran lives a few streets over from Main Street. Since I'm not carrying anything, it won't be a bad walk.

For a second, I think I should invite Hughes, maybe sneak in a make-out session, but I don't see him in the crowd as I grab my coat.

Main Street is bustling. The Jingle Bites Café is dark, though. If I had more cash flow—thanks a lot, Taylor

Grace—I could have hired someone to keep it open tonight. Now I'm losing revenue. Maybe it's better if it just fails.

Josie says Mace can get me another admin job at Svensson PharmaTech. Perhaps I just need to accept my lot in life.

*Or,* part of me whispers as I heave against the back door that I use to take deliveries, *maybe you and Hughes could get married and have babies, and you could stay home with them.*

It *does* sound nice to finally not have to lie awake at three in the morning, trying to figure out how to make payroll and conduct a UN-level negotiation with Taylor Grace to keep her from taking money out of the company.

I can't quite get the door to open. Did something fall behind it? I shove at the door with all my strength and hear something slide across the floor. I squeeze in through the crack in the door and fumble for the light switch. The LED light dims then powers up.

I blink in the bright light, then I see the hand and the pool of blood.

## CHAPTER 18

# Hughes

"Whoo! The strippers are here!"

Several elderly women whoop when the police walk into the living room.

The party is crazy. The Christmas punch is flowing. And Willow has disappeared.

Bobby tries to yell something over the thumping remixes of Christmas carols.

"What?" I yell at him.

Bobby yells something unintelligible.

"What? There's been a what?"

Someone pulls the plug to the music right as Bobby screams at the top of his lungs, "There's been a murder at the Jingle Bites Café! Taylor Grace is dead!"

The partygoers let out drunken gasps, then it's a free-for-all as people yell for their coats and stream out into the night, heading into town.

"A murder? Who murdered her?" I demand.

"We have the suspect in custody." Bobby sounds out of breath as we head to the café.

"It's probably the same person who murdered Jonah," Josie says, hurrying up next to me.

Mace Svensson runs after her with her coat, yelling, "Stay away from that crime scene, Josie, please!"

"Oh, go drink some hand sanitizer—you'll be fine!" she calls to her husband.

"Where is Willow?" I search the crowd. "She's going to want to see who the murderer is. Has anyone seen where she went?"

Bobby looks grim. "She'll be difficult to find, because the person we have in custody is Willow."

"What?" I stop short. "Willow didn't kill Taylor Grace."

"She was shot dead in Willow's café. The evidence begs to differ," Bobby tells me.

I shove my way through the crowd of people peering in through the windows of the Jingle Bites Café as, inside, the police conduct their investigation. An ambulance pulls up, and the EMTs start unpacking the stretcher.

Willow sits on one of the café seats, head in her hands.

Winston Girthman points at her. "Caught the murderer. It's always who you least expect."

"Willow didn't murder Taylor Grace—she's been at the Christmas party this whole time," I argue.

"The whole time? Because several people"—Bobby gestures to the crowd outside—"said they saw her leave twenty minutes ago."

"So she leaves the party, lures Taylor Grace here, and kills her? Then what? Calls the police? Doesn't go back to the party, doesn't just leave the body here and pretend to discover it in the morning?" I argue. "That doesn't make any sense."

"Don't talk to the cops!" Willow's grandmother rails, swatting at the police as she bursts into the café. "They don't want to do their jobs, so they go after my granddaughter. She's about to get married and have a baby—she's not out here murdering anyone!"

"You're getting married?" Nana exclaims, hugging me. "Oh, this is a wonderful Christmas!"

"If you'd caught the murderer earlier, then Taylor Grace would still be alive," I argue with Bobby.

"This isn't our fault!" the police argue with Nana.

I look around at the crowd gathered outside the café. The murderer has to be among them. I just don't believe that Willow killed Taylor Grace.

"You don't even have the murder weapon!" Nana shouts at Bobby, batting him with her handbag. "I'm this close to having great-grandbabies—you're not going to lock Willow up while her uterus is still functional."

I survey the crowd. Most people are a mix of shocked and horrified.

One elegant-looking woman has her arms wrapped around herself. There's a weird red patch on the white of her sweater under her arm, but I don't dwell on it because two people here look neither shocked nor upset. Lydia is arguing with her husband, Travis. Neither of them seems at all concerned that Taylor Grace is dead, I notice.

Hollis appears, tears streaming down her face as she wraps an arm around Lylia.

I open the door to gesture them inside.

"Is the body still in there?" Hollis asks, voice trembling. "I don't know if Lydia needs to see this. Lydia's in shock, aren't you?"

"Oh, bring her inside, poor thing," Beryl tuts.

"She's pregnant! You're stressing out a pregnant woman!" Nana snaps at Bobby.

"I'll go get you some water," I tell Lydia as her husband helps her into a seat.

The police look longingly at the stacks of pastries for tomorrow.

"Willow won't mind if you have one," I tell them.

While they're distracted, making their choices, I survey the crime scene. There's a smear of blood on the floor where Willow shoved the door open. Taylor Grace looks like she was killed right before Willow arrived—shot by a small-caliber weapon, a pistol, three times in the back.

Had she been arguing with someone then turned to leave? Or had she been ambushed?

I notice a phone half hidden next to the spice rack on one of the counters. It's blush pink. I swipe it and stick it in my pocket before the police see.

"Any sign of a murder weapon?" I ask as I slowly fill a glass of water.

"No." The police shrug.

"Did you check the dumpster outside?"

Bobby snaps his fingers. "Good idea. You should be a detective on the force." He beams at me.

I let the EMTs come through then head back into the café.

Lydia is being comforted by Josie.

"It was a delayed reaction from the shock."

"Dead. She's dead. My sister is dead. Taylor Grace's dead." Lydia sobs as I set the water down near her.

Her husband looks angry.

"Do you have any idea who might have killed her?" I ask.

"Yeah," her husband says.

"No," Lydia snaps at him.

"Yes, we do." He's stubborn.

The police fumble out their notepads. Winston drops his tape recorder. The firemen, who've been called for crowd control, roll their eyes.

"She did it." Travis points at Willow.

"Me?" she cries. "I would never!"

"You stand to gain the most from her death. No, Lydia, we have to tell them," Travis says, cutting her off. "Taylor Grace was trying to regain control of her company."

"Not regain control—she was trying to steal it from Willow! Willow did all the work," Josie argues. "Taylor stole from her."

"Well, now Willow gets the company scot-free," Travis says nastily.

"Yeah, and all the debt," Willow snaps. "It's not like I'm making out like a bandit here."

"Willow did it. She found the body. Why did you disappear from the party?" Lydia's husband demands.

"I had to get the maple bacon twists."

"Very convenient!" Travis shouts.

"I was about to go get them," Josie argues. "Why are you so intent on blaming this on Willow, huh? Maybe you killed Taylor, and you're trying to throw people off the trail."

The husband sputters. "Me? I was at the party."

"Were you?" Josie shouts.

"Just, please. Taylor Grace is dead. Can we do this another time? I can't—" Lydia holds a fluttering hand to her head.

"You're stressing her out." Hollis comforts Lydia.

I glare at Travis, who doesn't look sorry.

"Besides," Nana says stubbornly, "everyone knows it's always the wronged husband."

The police look confused.

"Taylor Grace was having an affair. Don't ask."

They nod along.

"Bobby, are you investigating Damien?" I ask.

"No? He was the high school football championship team's QB. He's the nephew of the police chief. We can't just go investigating him for no reason," he protests.

"So you haven't even questioned him?" I raise an eyebrow.

"He's innocent until proven guilty," he whines.

"You're not even trying to prove guilt. You're just letting him walk!" I raise my voice.

"Ding-dong, the bitch is dead!" Damien bursts in drunkenly, raising a glass as he stumbles around. "And I killed her!" He leans over like he's bowing. Then he collapses on the floor of the café.

"Well." Bobby flips his notepad closed. "Guess that ends both investigations. We have a confession, boys!"

# CHAPTER 19

# Willow

"I did what?" Damien groans next to me in the cell the next morning. We've spent all night crammed in a cell with a number of seniors who came for their annual holiday pilgrimage from Florida and were singing Christmas carols drunkenly. "I ain't killed nobody."

"Me neither!" I protest. "Damien confessed. Why am I here?"

"Didn't," Damien slurs.

"You're an accomplice, Willow. And we have a video of you confessing," the cops explain.

"The police in this town are incompetent!" I screech and rattle the bars.

The worst part? The murderer is long gone with their bloody coat from Gran's house.

Damien leans over to puke.

"We also," interjects the police chief, a big, burly man with a bad sunburn and an even worse attitude, "have several witnesses to you wandering the Christmas market, screaming your head off about how your wife was cheating on you and was trying to steal your money."

"She is trying to steal my money, Uncle! You need to tell Taylor Grace that I started the divorce proceedings. I want a restraining order against her—and the guy she's cheating on me with."

"Dr. Merriweather," I tell the police chief, filling him in.

Damien wrinkles his nose.

The police chief swears. "Well, both of them are dead."

"Wait, Taylor is actually dead? Like, you're not just fucking with me? Uncle Ralph, my wife is dead?" Damien sits heavily on the floor.

"Now don't cry, pet," one of the elderly women says to him as he buries his face in his hands. "My husband keeled over dead one day in the '80s, and it was the best thing that ever happened to me."

Chewing on a toothpick, the police chief glares down at Damien, then he grunts. Does he think Damien is innocent? "Willow. Your bail's been posted. You're free to go. You cannot," he warns, "leave town. Can't believe this shit. I leave town for five days—I have a five-day vacation—and it all goes to shit."

I follow him out into the chilly lobby.

Hughes wraps me up in a hug. "Are you all right?" He cups my face. "I tried to get you out sooner. They wouldn't let me, even though Nana said they usually take bribes."

"Wait, you bailed me out?" My eyes search his.

"The amount they're charging for bail these days!" His grandmother is horrified.

"They upped it because of the Christmas season."

"This town is run by the Mafia!" Nana shakes her fist in the direction of the police chief, who looks like he would rather be anywhere but dealing with the general public.

"He sprung you out of jail." Gran tries to wipe at my face. "You need to let him hit that, girlie. Man puts up that much bail money, he should get to open as many Advent calendar doors as he wants. You feel me?" She swats my hip. "Go get 'em."

"You probably want to go home," Hughes tells me. He still looks concerned.

"Can't," Gran states. "The new Airbnb-ers are there. They want their dog to stay in your shed. You'll have to stay at Mary Lou's carriage house." My grandmother winks at me. "I'm your best wingwoman."

"I should, um..." After a murder and a night in jail, I really just want a shower, but is that weird? I mean, getting naked with just a door between me and the guy I like seems like a big step to make on no sleep. "I really need to go clean my shop. I need to get it open again. I can't keep hemorrhaging money."

"Well, thankfully, Taylor Grace is dead, so you don't have to."

There is a small crowd outside my shop when I walk up, Hughes protectively beside me. I pull at the caution tape over the door and step inside. Instead of the smell of freshly baked cookies, it smells like death.

"I don't think I can do this." I slump into a chair.

"Let me make you some tea. Peppermint?"

"Black tea. I need some caffeine," I groan.

The kettle boils.

"Willow," Hughes says then waits a beat.

"What?"

"Never mind. I just wanted to ask you, well..." He trails off.

"What?" I snap at him. "You think I did it? You think I killed Taylor Grace?"

"No, that's not—I was going to ask you if you were okay staying with me tonight in the carriage house."

I immediately feel bad for being mean.

*This is why you're alone...*

"So," I whisper, "you don't think I'm a murderer?"

"Even if you are," he whispers, "I still want to kiss you. I wanted to kiss you last night."

"Do you think an overnight is a little too soon? We haven't even held hands yet."

He leans in, lacing his fingers with mine. "I think we can fix that."

And then he does—slowly at first, tentatively, like we're testing the edges of something dangerous. His hand finds my jaw, thumb tracing along my cheek, anchoring me in the quiet chaos of the moment. For one suspended second, the world narrows to the heat of his mouth and the wild hammering of my heart.

When we finally break apart, he whispers, "You never actually said that you definitely didn't kill your business partner. Still think I should be worried?"

"Only if you stop kissing me," I say and pull him back in. I press kisses to his mouth and jaw. "For the record, I did not kill Taylor Grace. Not that I haven't bought a voodoo doll or two, hoping the universe will take her out."

He laughs, nuzzling my nose with his. Giddy from the lack of sleep and the feeling of being in his arms, I wrap my arms around his neck.

"Oh!" Hollis stands wide-eyed in the doorway. "I didn't realize you were..."

"Um..." I jump back from Hughes.

He still keeps my hand in his.

"Just, uh..."

"I'm here to clean up," Hollis says, her eyes red and puffy.

"You don't have to do that."

"I—I feel like I should. I—" She sounds like she's about to cry.

"There's a lot of blood. I'll take care of it. You should go home." I shoo her to the door. "Rose is at the stall."

"I can't just sit at home," Hollis frets. "I just—I don't understand how this happened. And the police don't know anything. They can't find her phone, and they aren't even trying to solve this case."

"Maybe we should just let well enough alone," Hughes says. "As long as we can prove Willow didn't do it, then what's the problem?"

Hollis gives him a long look. "Yeah, I guess so. I'll take the last of the sugarplum truffles to the stall," she tells me, grabbing a napkin to wipe her eyes.

I lock the door behind her.

Hughes starts filling a bucket with soapy water.

As soon as we're alone, he kisses me again, right there next to the ovens.

I'm boiling up by the time he releases me.

"I probably should shower before, um..." I pull at my sweater.

"Before I eat your Christmas cookies?" He smirks. Then he dunks a mop into the bucket and starts mopping the floor.

I poke around half-heartedly for cleaning supplies, the tea not doing as much caffeine-wise as I need to wake up.

"So, who do you think killed her?" he asks as I grab a broom and sweep under the counters. The police have tracked in all sorts of leaves. "I mean, I think Lydia was acting weird last night."

"She wouldn't kill her own sister, would she?" I wonder.

"Could be Lydia's husband. My money's on Damien, though."

"He says he didn't do it." I fill him in on the conversation in the jail cell.

Something metallic clinks on the floor. I almost shout at Hughes to come look, but something stops me. Maybe it's Hollis's reaction to him. Maybe it's how he doesn't seem upset that Taylor Grace, his client, is gone. Maybe it's best to play things close to the vest.

"I'm going to dump this water in the drain outside," Hughes tells me, hefting the bucket.

I nod, watching him leave, then quickly bend down to investigate. It's not a piece of metal or a mixer attachment. It's a bracelet. I don't think I've seen Taylor Grace wear anything like it. It looks expensive—a diamond glitters on it. It's a delicate piece, the diamond hanging off the chain like a little charm. Does it belong to the murderer? Are we looking for a woman? If so, she's a very elegant one.

Then I notice the smell. It's spicy, pungent, almost tart. These aren't leaves from the trees outside. They're something else. I grab a handful and wrap them in a napkin along with the bracelet. I stick them in my pocket right as Hughes comes in, shaking off the snow.

"Find any clues?" Hughes asks with a smile.

I pull him down for a kiss so I don't have to look into his eyes when I lie. "No."

# CHAPTER 20

# Hughes

I'd rather be kissing Willow, but I have a case to solve. Seeing her hauled off to jail lit something in me. They aren't going to take my girl away from me.

Mine? Yeah.

And someone clearly was trying to frame her with this murder. Did the murderer lure Taylor Grace to the shop to shoot her? I would bet money on it. As it is, I'm betting my freedom and professional reputation on it.

I spent all night modifying a code I wrote a couple of years ago to crack into a phone. And it's finally ready to go. First, I test it on an iPhone of a similar make and model. Now, I'm going to crack Taylor Grace's cell phone. I hum with satisfaction. It isn't supposed to be possible. But I've made a pretty good living out of doing impossible things with computers.

I plug in Taylor Grace's phone and run the code. While my hard drive churns, I stand to pace around the open kitchen and living area of the carriage house.

Willow is coming here tonight. I need to make everything perfect.

The door flies open.

"Nana, you can't just barge in here. What if Willow were here?"

"I've been watching the house. I know you don't have a woman in here." She bustles in, carrying a big basket.

"Her granny and I put our heads together." She hands me the box of condoms. "Now go try one of these on."

"I have my own condoms." I hand them back to her.

She glares at me. "I don't need you to mess this up for me and Willow's granny. We've got a lot invested in this relationship. And now that Taylor Grace has gone to the great tanning salon in the sky, Willow should be all mentally freed up to date you. You can't blow it tonight. You want to give her the D. Don't give her the L."

"I really don't want to have this conversation with you, ever."

"It's a public service." She pulls a dildo out of the basket.

"This is what Willow's grandmother got her last year, so she should be very familiar, in case you can't, you know…" She makes a noise like air getting let out of a balloon.

"I really don't think I'll have a problem, but I'm sure Willow's going to love this curated sex toy collection from a close family member."

Nana beams. "Tell her she's very welcome."

I stuff the basket under the sink in the bathroom, making a mental note to retrieve it before any new Airbnb guests come.

Then, I stare at my murder wall and add the printout of Lydia and her husband. It's always a loved one, right? Or the person one would most suspect. Willow does have a lot to gain from this murder.

"Shut up," I tell the ceiling. It's the wannabe PI in me. But I'm evolving. I wear a puffer jacket now. Maybe I'll start getting into woodworking or meat smoking.

I probably should put a photo of Nana and Beryl on the board, but if my granny is a murderer, I really do not want to know.

I check Taylor Grace's phone. The code is running and will run for a while longer as it works to break into the iPhone.

I lay back on the couch and try to think through the murder.

I really need a permanent workspace. There's shared office space available in the city, but maybe I should buy a house—after the Christmas season is over, of course. I wonder what kind of house Willow would like. I scroll through Zillow.

There's a nice Victorian with a big yard and a carriage house out back. Probably would be a great yard for kids—nice and flat. Kids. With Willow. Yeah, that would be nice.

The phone beeps. Done already? I get a high when one of my codes works. But breaking into an iPhone?

"Man, I'm good," I crow when I see the phone's contents splayed out on the screen in front of me.

I type another command, then the phone is copied onto my hard drive.

"And we make an extra copy because you can't have too many backups. Done." I carefully wipe down the phone for fingerprints and wrap it in a tissue.

I can't have the phone on me. I'll dump it in the Christmas market and let some tourist turn it in to the cops. I don the trench coat to venture out. I'm dumping evidence of a murder, after all. I have to look the part.

It's a little warmer in the market with all the tourists packed in and the various fires going. The smell of smoke, roasted chestnuts, and spiced wine fills the air.

I've left my phone at the carriage house so it can't track me as I make my way through the market to a more remote area.

I work my fingers into the pocket of my trench coat—the pocket that I've cut—and push the phone through while I'm walking by a stall, pretending like I'm shopping for my holiday sweetheart. The phone thunks into the snow with barely a sound. Done. Now it's time to find Willow.

I turn a corner, thinking I can take a shortcut back to the carriage house. Then, suddenly, I'm in a dark part of the market. The temperature drops, and I pull my trench coat around me, hunching my shoulders.

Over the whistling of the wind, I faintly hear someone cry, "Help!"

# CHAPTER 21

# Willow

An earring, a bracelet, and odd-smelling leaves. All clues from two different murder scenes near or at places that I own.

"What does it mean?" I whisper to the items laid out on the counter of the shop. I'm waiting for the last batch of cookies to finish baking so I can take them to the Christmas market stall.

Could someone be trying to frame me? Why are both murders connected to me? Not to mention the only person who would have any logical reason to frame me is currently in the morgue.

I pack the cookies into a basket, drape it with a towel, and head out into the Christmas market.

I'll open the shop tomorrow. I guess.

All while in business with Taylor Grace, I fantasized about quitting, about running away to Tokyo or something and just leaving the business to rot. Now that she's out of the picture? Well, this might just be a merry Christmas after all.

"I really shouldn't be so evil," I remind myself.

Taylor Grace was my friend before she showed her true colors. Thinking ill of the dead could come back to bite me.

Still guilty, I start mentally calculating the numbers now that I don't have to pay her any more money.

"I'm free!"

Around me, I hear whispers, feel the stares.

Realizing I'm smiling, I force myself to look, not sad—that might be a stretch—but at least unhappy. I don't want the townspeople to think I've committed a double homicide.

Rose is in the stall. "Oh my gosh, perfect!" she squeals when I set the cookies on the counter. "I was about to get eaten alive by influencers."

I stare down at the case.

Rose giggles.

"I made a little change and upped the prices."

"Murder Munchies cookie?" I read the card.

"We didn't have that many, so it's supply and demand." Rose flips her hair.

"Double Chocolate Homicide?" I groan. "People are going to think that we had something to do with the murder—that I had something to do with it."

"Everyone else is profiting off of it, and now that Taylor Grace is gone—praise the queen of karma herself!" Rose rummages through the cookies. "I'm calling these Willow's Revenge."

"No, you are not."

A headache is settling behind my eyes as I step back out into the snowy Christmas market. This is getting out of hand. I have to find some more clues, more evidence to point me in the direction of the murderer. But first I need something to eat.

After waiting in line for thirty minutes—gasp—I have a piping hot Mistletoe Melt. The thick-cut rosemary sourdough, buttered and grilled golden, holds Brie cheese, cranberry chutney, and roasted turkey breast hash with a drizzle of aioli.

My first stop is the jewelry stalls.

Actually, my first stop is one of the apple cider stalls. Sipping the steaming hot drink, I plot out what I'm going to say to weasel some information out of one of the jewelers.

After cosplaying an interested customer, I spy a jeweler who has wares most similar to the bracelet I've found. I hover, waiting for the customers to trail out, then I approach the counter.

"Hi!" I try to sound bubbly. "I wanted to see if you knew who might be able to make a bracelet like one I borrowed from a friend." I fumble the chain out and extend it on my mitten.

"Where did you get this?" the stall owner demands.

"Um—"

"It's a custom piece. For a billionaire. I made this for Mace Svensson. It is very expensive. How do you have it?" she demands.

I tuck my chin down into the scarf. "Oh, well, yes, I am friends with his wife, so—"

"If you were already friends with her, why do you need to ask around to see who crafted it?" The jewelry stall owner doesn't seem convinced. "I'm calling the Christmas cops."

"No need!" I yelp. "I'm actually going to go meet her now. Bye!"

I jog out of the stall then run blindly through the crowd, dodging a Christmas cop on a big horse snorting in the cold and almost running into a lady selling Christmas cheer cups from a small cart.

"Watch it!"

"Sorry, Noelle."

I keep jogging, though not very far. I lurch to a stop and double over next to a stall, coughing and out of breath, hoping that no Christmas cops are after me. I suck in air. I really shouldn't have eaten that sandwich before trying to do physical exertion. Ah, who am I kidding? I'm just generally out of shape.

I peer at the ground. Another dead end. Josie is forgetful. *She must have dropped the bracelet in my shop.* But why hasn't she asked about it? She has a lot of jewelry. She probably didn't realize.

Mace, though—he's meticulous. He's always watching after her. He would notice if she left with a bracelet then didn't come home with it. When she and I are out, he often comes by with something Josie's forgotten.

"It's a mistake or a misunderstanding," I tell myself firmly.

Josie's not the murderer, right?

*She was late to the party…*

"She's not a murderer. I'm hungry and tired. Well, maybe not that hungry." I suck in air through my nose, trying not to sound like I'm dying, when I smell it—a familiar, pungent, spicy, sour, herby smell. Just like the leaves I found in my shop. Sniffing the air, I follow the smell through the market.

There are fewer tourists in this part of the market, farther from the ice rink and oversized Christmas tree. I plod along slowly, trying not to lose the thread of the scent. Is it coming from someplace closer to the Main Street market entrance or by the general store?

"*...be thankful that she's gone*," a man says in a low voice.

I carefully step toward the little pocket seating area festooned with Christmas garlands and trees and tiny tables with candles in glass vases.

"*...can't let anyone find out. We'll go to jail forever.*"

"*...one will find out...*"

"*...she had it coming... good she's dead.*"

I peer around a Christmas tree and see Lydia and her husband, heads bent.

Oh my god. I back away, trying to disappear as quickly and quietly as possible back into the warren of Christmas market stalls. Did they kill Taylor Grace? Are Lydia and her husband the murderers? But what about Jonah?

Maybe Lydia was pissed Jonah was enabling Taylor Grace, they got into an argument, Travis came to her rescue, and bam—Jonah was dead. Travis is strong enough to hoist Jonah's body. Then Taylor Grace went even crazier, and bang—she died too. But Travis has a good job at Svensson PharmaTech. Would he really risk it all to murder someone?

Maybe Lydia murdered her sister, and Travis just covered it up. I don't know. I've never been in love. But I wonder if a man could ever love me enough to cover up a murder for me.

I'm lost in thought. Then it hits me. The smell. So pungent it makes me sneeze. I don't have any trouble following it to a small storage shed at the back of a stall. Heart pounding, I check the door. It's unlocked. I ease it open. I'm just going to stick my head inside...

"Aah!"

Someone shoves me, and I fall in, scraping my hands.

"Hey!" Scrambling up, I rush to the door, push, kick, try to get it open. But it's locked. Dammit.

The murderer—it has to be. Was it Travis and Lydia? Did they see me?

I scroll through my phone. I don't want to call 911 and tip the murderers off that I'm onto them. I call Hughes. No answer. Then I call Josie. No answer. Gran? No answer.

"Why doesn't anyone answer their phone?" I fume, giving the door another kick.

Then I smell something burning…

# CHAPTER 22
# Hughes

“*Help!*” I hear again, faint over the wind.

It takes me a second to figure out where the cries are coming from as I turn through the twisting, narrow pathways of stalls crammed into the Christmas market.

“*Help!*”

I’m closer now, and I smell the smoke of something burning. I turn down a small alley behind the narrow rows of stalls.

A figure all in black slams into my shoulder as he runs past me.

“Hey!” I call out to him.

It’s dark. I can’t get a good look at him—just a flash of heavy black boots and canvas work pants. I have to make a decision: Follow the guy, or help whoever is calling for it? I race after the perp. Hoofbeats thud on the gravel path, and I'm almost mowed over by a huge black horse.

"Hey!" I wave down one of the Christmas cops. "Did you see a guy run past here? I think he hurt someone," I tell them urgently.

One of them looks at the other, a big bushy-bearded man. "Remy, you want to do the honors?"

I don't wait to see if they follow the perp. I just race back to follow the cries for help.

They're coming from a stall painted all black with weird sigils all over it.

"Help!"

"Willow? Willow!"

"Hughes!"

I step back, take two steps, then kick in the door. Wood splits. I kick it again, then the metal latch breaks off the wood, and the door slams open.

"Oh my god! Willow!" I gather her to my chest. "Are you all right?"

"I think so." Her voice is muffled against my chest.

I squeeze her to me, kissing her hair, her cheeks. I cup her face. "What happened? How'd you get locked in here?"

"I don't know. I was investigating and—" She looks around wildly. "I have so much to tell you."

"Okay, come home where it's warm." I take off my trench coat and wrap it around her.

"I'm really fine. I promise."

A black cat crosses in front of our path and yowls eerily.

"I think I've had enough Christmas market for one day." Willow shivers.

"Funny, because we didn't say you could leave," someone says.

Two black-haired twins materialize out of thin air.

"You broke my sister's stall," one of them says.

"Yes, and you need to repair it."

I look back at the busted door.

"I'm a computer software engineer, not a woodworker. Can I just pay you for damages?"

"You can come work at the stall to pay off your debt," the twins say as one.

"You don't take cryptocurrency?" I grimace.

"Money is the root of all evil," the left one states flatly.

"I can give you gold galleons…"

They stare blankly.

"Fine, indentured servitude it is."

Horses snort, then the huge animals round the corner, half dragging a man in black with them.

"Damien?" Willow says, shocked. "You're the killer?"

"The what?" the man squawks.

The Christmas cops glare down at him.

"Remy, you need to arrest him," I tell the bearded man hotly. "He shoved my girlfriend into a shed, locked her in, and set it on fire."

"Another fire, Lilith?" Remy sighs.

"It wasn't burning," one of the black-haired twins states, unblinking. "We were making a witch's potion."

Remy shakes his head. "Y'all aren't supposed to be having unpermitted bonfires in the market."

"It's ambience. Besides"—as one, the twins stare down at Damien—"our cauldron is conveniently large enough to boil a murderer. Alive."

"I swear," Damien babbles, "I didn't lock her in the shed."

Morticia pulls out a long, thin stiletto blade.

"I swear on my life." Damien falls to his knees.

"Yes, you did, and you killed Taylor Grace and Jonah Merriweather because they were having an affair," Willow says accusingly.

"I didn't kill my wife."

"She was your soon-to-be ex-wife, and there are multiple instances of the two of you arguing in public. Your pending divorce was contentious. You're the jealous type."

"I never—" Damien chokes out.

"He locked her in the stall. At least arrest him for that." I point at the ruined shed.

Damien sets his jaw. "This is bullshit. I didn't lock up nobody."

"Then why were you over here?"

"I was looking for Willow, but"—he babbles before I can castrate him—"I didn't want to lock her in the shed. I need to talk to her."

"Uh-huh." The Christmas cops don't look like they're buying it.

"Yeah, because I want to know how to get my half of the shop." Damien nods.

"Your half of the—"

I have to grab Willow around the waist before she launches herself at Damien, who runs to hide behind Remy.

"That isn't your shop. That's my shop!" she shrieks.

"Taylor Grace owned half the shop. She told me. And now that she's dead, it's mine," Damien bellows while Willow tries to struggle out of my grasp.

"You don't even know how to bake! You don't know how to run a business! You have a gambling problem, and you eat microwave burritos from the gas station."

"Do you have any paperwork that says it's half hers?" Remy asks.

"She and Willow had a verbal agreement that Willow reneged on." Damien is stubborn.

"Fine," Willow spits, eyes flashing. "You want half the shop? Have it. We're twenty thousand dollars in debt, thanks to your wife, so that means half of that debt is yours. You need to pay me ten thousand dollars immediately."

"I—what?" Damien's face wrinkles. "Taylor Grace said you had lots of money coming in."

"We do not. She has been taking a salary because she claimed that her creative energy was keeping the stall afloat—spoiler, it wasn't. So we need a cash infusion." Willow holds out her hand. "Pay up. Now. Oh, and you're taking the 4 a.m. shift, so I expect to see you at the kitchen bright and early in, oh, seven and a half hours."

Damien blanches. "That's awful early."

"Running a business is work," Remy tells him. "Sounds like you have a second job. Congratulations."

"Why don't we all go to the bank right now?" Willow's face is splotchy. "And you can go ahead and withdraw that money from your bank account. That will help us make payroll."

"Well, never mind," Damien mumbles.

"No, I insist," Willow says hotly. "You're right. It is half yours now. The Harrogate Community Bank should still be open."

"I don't want any part of that business. It's not mine, and I don't want any creditors breaking down my door about it." Damien backs away. "You can have it. I'm not setting foot in that shop or giving you a dollar."

Remy taps his body cam and winks at Willow. “Maybe you know a computer person who can download this for posterity’s sake.”

# CHAPTER 23

# Willow

"I'm too tired to eat." I slump into a chair in the carriage house living room.

On the coffee table, Hughes sets down the pizza and the Yuletide beer that smells suspiciously like repurposed pumpkin spice beer from the fall festival.

"At least you don't smell like a jail cell anymore." He kisses the top of my wet hair and pours the beer into a mug. "The guy at the craft brewing stall said it needed to be served warm."

"Warm beer will send me over the edge." I accept the piping hot pizza that is fortunately holiday themed only because of the tomato and pesto and not because someone did something unholy with the recipe. I sip the beer then take a bite of the hot pizza, the herbs a jolt on my tongue.

I set the mug painted with jolly Santas on my knee and look at the whiteboard in front of me, on which Hughes is moving Damien's photo to the "cleared" column.

"We don't actually know that he's not the murderer," I remind him.

"He's never actually said he wants her dead. He seems lazy and entitled. He didn't lock you in the stall." Hughes turns to me.

"That's just what he said. We don't know." I take another bite of pizza.

"There are others who are more likely suspects than he is." Hughes refills my mug.

"He's not off the board completely. So, who else do we have?" I glare.

"There's Josie—"

"Josie did not kill Taylor!" I yell.

"You said you found her bracelet," he argues. "If you want Damien to be a suspect, then Josie needs to be one too."

"Put her in the cleared column. In fact, take her off the board entirely."

"Where was she the night of the Christmas party?" Hughes presses.

"Off the board." I gesture with the mug.

He sighs and puts her photo on a chair. "I guess you want our grannies off the board too?"

I point.

Their photos are taken down.

"So, who are we left with?"

"Mysterious earring owner, Maris, the person in black who locked you in the stall."

"Lydia and her husband," I add.

Hughes stares at the photos. "This is Maris?" He taps her photo.

"Yup."

"Huh."

"What?"

"The night of Taylor Grace's murder… I saw her with what I now wonder might have been a bloodstain on her sweater."

"The bloody coat," I say to fill him in.

"Damn. I mean, she's a suspect, then. Maris Dupuis? Taylor Grace ruined her business and ran her out of town. She mysteriously comes back a few weeks before Taylor Grace is killed?" Hughes lets out a low whistle. "But who on this list would want to kill both Taylor Grace and Dr. Merriweather?"

"Maybe it's two completely different murderers and they're unrelated. Or—" I snap my fingers. "Maybe Lenore and Maris did a murder swap, like Maris killed Jonah and Lenore killed Taylor Grace, so they both have alibis and they both win."

"Or—" Hughes puts Damien's photo back on the wall. "We look at the people who have reason to kill both."

I add Lenore's photo. "These two are directly impacted by the affair and have the most to gain."

"Damien doesn't gain anything," Hughes argues.

"But he thought he'd gain half a business. Don't any of these people have alibis?" I ask.

"Maybe." He pulls up his computer on the large TV on one wall. "I've written a script to troll the Harrogate tags on Facebook to see if we can pick up anyone. I ran it after Dr. Merriweather's murder, and of course, everyone on this list was in the Christmas market and at the tree lighting during the time of the murder, so no alibi."

I try not to be too impressed.

"And the night of Taylor Grace's murder?" Hughes scrolls through the results that the program turned up. "Most of these people were at the Christmas party, though they could have murdered Taylor Grace right before or snuck out during the event."

"We don't have an exact time of death?"

"The coroner seemed overwhelmed when I brought him some sympathy jerky. He kept bitching that the mayor wanted him to perform the autopsy right now."

"Is he really that backed up? How many deaths have happened in Harrogate?"

"Nope. He's been renting out the morgue to Airbnb-ers and doesn't want to evict them yet because he'll be out the money."

"This freaking town," I mutter.

"Lenore posted that she was at home, which could have been fake. And Damien doesn't show up in the photos, though that doesn't mean he is in the clear."

"Okay, move Damien back to the suspect side. Wait—" I hold up a hand as I type into my phone. "No, he's clear."

"What?"

I hold up my phone.

"#DrunksOfHgate?" Hughes reads the hashtag name.

"There's Damien." I point at a man lying next to a stall, his pants undone—while a tourist mugs for the camera to take a selfie.

"Maybe he went and drank after he killed Taylor Grace," Hughes argues. "If anything, this is more evidence in my column. He stays a suspect."

I glare at him. He's staring at my chest.

I look down. Do a double take. "Crap." I pull the robe closed. "Sorry, didn't mean to flash you."

"Oh yeah." His voice is deliciously deep. "Because I kind of hoped you were coming on to me." He hooks three fingers on the robe and tugs it away.

And then I have a cute guy staring at my bare chest.

He licks his lips and leans in. His breath is hot on my skin. "I'm going to assume—" His head moves up, lips barely caressing my flesh until his mouth is just a hair's breadth away from mine. "That you aren't wearing any panties under that robe."

"Unh," I make a strangled noise and am glad he starts kissing me before he notices and doesn't want me anymore.

I grab his hair as he breaks the kiss, moves down my body to tug at the tie of my robe. It falls open, then he's spreading my legs. I squeak when suddenly his mouth is right there, and his tongue is on me and in me, and I'm rocking against his face as he licks me like a candy cane until I'm riding that sinful tongue all the way to the *Nutcracker* fairyland. Sugarplums, Christmas cookies on fire. I know I'm gushing all over him as he licks me clean.

"Wow, that, um—" I swallow.

He looks up, smirking. "You want to take a break from solving a murder?"

I make a strangled noise. "That sounds scary crazy."

"So you don't want—" Hughes gives me a quizzical look.

Figures—the one time I get a man, I completely blow it. "Just give me a second." I scoot around him then stub my toe on the coffee table as I rush into the bathroom.

What in the Christmas hell? Did I seriously just have Hughes's tongue in my you-know-where? And now we're, what, going to have sex on the couch?

I pace in the tiny bathroom. "You can have sex. You're overthinking this. People have sex."

I look down. In my post-orgasm clarity, I have to wonder, after all my holiday stress eating, is this really what a guy wants to see? Like, I'm going to have to take the whole robe off.

I'm freaking out for no reason. It's just a hookup. People hook up. Gran hooks up.

I shudder and open up the cupboards, looking for a washcloth or alcohol. Instead, I find—

"What the hell is this?"

# CHAPTER 24
# Hughes

*Dammit*. "Look, Willow," I say when she stomps out of the bathroom, basket in one hand, dildo in the other.

"Is this some sort of weird fetish thing? Did you steal this out of my shed?"

"Your grandmother bought you a new one. She wanted to make sure you had something you were familiar with." I swallow.

"Oh God," Willow groans, sinking onto the couch. "This is a disaster. I'd say I need to go home, but I can't!"

"Hey, if you want to get out of sleeping with me, no problem." I smirk. "I'm sure I can scrounge you a hotel room somewhere. Though we might have to go to the next town over. I'll just jack off later, thinking about your tits."

Two spots color her cheeks. She sputters, "That's not what I'm trying to do."

"Really?" I lean over her on the couch. "Don't you want to unwrap my Christmas present?" I press a kiss to her neck.

"Mm-hm," she moans.

I lean down to suck on one pink nipple. I'm rock-hard at how her breathing intensifies, turning into pants just from my tongue.

"Give me a white Christmas," she moans, reaching for my pants.

I groan when she touches the bulge in my boxer briefs, grab her hair when she mouths against the fabric.

"Where do you want your white Christmas?" I can barely get the words out.

"I'll show you." She pulls down the boxer briefs.

Her hand is perfect as she runs her thumb along the tip, twists her grip, licks the tip of my cock, takes it in her mouth, then finally squeezes me between her perfect tits.

I grip the back of the couch, lost in the sound of her, the feel of her.

"I'm dreaming," she sings slightly off-key, "of a white"—she squeezes her tits around me—"Christmas."

She sighs as I explode all over her chest and chin.

"Come to bed," I beg her once I can string two words together. I lean in, kiss her mouth, her breasts…

"Wait…" She's staring up at the board. "Where is the list of all the people from Jonah's therapy practice?" she demands, pushing me off.

It takes a full minute for my brain to make its way sluggishly from my dick to my head. "Uhhh…"

"Focus." She snaps her fingers.

"A really tall order." My eyes are glued to her tits.

She huffs and closes the robe.

"I mean, is it really pertinent that we solve this murder?" I pull out the digitized list we made and search for Maris's name. "Nothing. Can we please go to bed now?"

"No." Her eyes narrow. "I'm missing something... Search for my name?"

"What?"

"Taylor Grace made me go do a few therapy sessions with her and Dr. Merriweather when I was trying way too hard to, quote, 'make things work and be understanding and hear her and leave space for her trauma,' unquote."

"You're not listed," I tell her.

"Search for Taylor's name."

I type it in dutifully. "There are tons."

"Where are the July dates?"

I scroll through. "There. It says, 'Taylor Grace and guest.'"

"Search for 'guest.'" She peers over my shoulder. "There, August two years ago. It has to be Maris. They were still in business together then. Taylor Grace probably made her go too." Willow claps her hands. "You don't understand," she says to my look of confusion. "Taylor Grace and Dr. Merriweather use it as a way to gang up on you, gaslight you, make you feel small and stupid. It was a horrible experience, and it was the beginning of the end for us. I had Josie to help me through. But Maris? I bet she hated Dr. Merriweather just as much as I did." Willow stands up. "We need to go find her."

"Where is she? Who knows where she's staying? With all the tourists, it'll be difficult to sort out."

"I know who knows," Willow says firmly.

"Who?"

"Lenore."

It's dark as we walk through town. A few drunks are stumbling around, doing their best to make the hall of fame on #DrunksOfHgate, and a few lost tourists stop to ask us for directions to their Airbnbs.

Lenore's huge house is dark.

"We can't just wake her up," I hiss.

"Maris could be staying here. Let's just look in the bedrooms. We can climb up the porch roof around back," Willow whispers. "Come on."

I curse and run after her around the side of the house then stop short when we see a dark figure standing over a bubbling cauldron, the flames licking the big black pot as a woman—*a witch!*—tosses leaves into the pot.

"*Bubble, bubble, spark and flame,*" the witch chants. "*Whisper softly the cursed name. Ashes fall and shadows creep. Bind the secret, dark and deep.*" The witch points her wand at us. "Hark! Who goes there? Speak, evil demons!"

"Um..." Willow holds up her hands. "We're just here to check that you have an adequate amount of Christmas cheer."

"Are you fuckers from the homeowners association? I swear to God—" The witch pulls her hood back, and Lenore glares at us. "My husband just died, and there's snow all over everything. You can't even see the grass. Oh, Willow, you work for the HOA now? Sold your soul, I see."

"Er, no, just here trying to figure out what happened to Taylor Grace." Willow grimaces. "The cops are all over me."

"You too? Yeah, they're after me as well. I'm like, you all waste so much taxpayer money, and yet the coroner still hasn't actually done an autopsy on Jonah. It's a scam they're running down at city hall," Lenore complains.

"Yeah, so we just wanted to see if Maris was here?"

"Now, why would she be here?" Lenore taps her wand on the cauldron.

"Well, you said she was a family friend."

"Yeah, she's at her grandmother's house. She's helping manage her Airbnb guests. I should probably rent this house out," Lenore muses. "Jonah hated the Airbnb-ing. He was constantly calling the Christmas committee on people. It was so obnoxious."

"Where does her grandmother live?" I ask.

"What, is he on something?" Lenore asks Willow, jerking her wand in my direction. "You dropped off Christmas treats at Mrs. Locke's house earlier this week. I had one of your granny's chocolate tarts. Amazing. I'd ask for the recipe, but I'm the worst cook."

Back out on the street, Willow is deep in thought.

"Guess we're going to Mrs. Locke's house," I say uncertainly.

Willow makes a noncommittal noise. She's scrolling on her phone.

My stomach sinks. I thought what we'd shared earlier was the best thing ever, better than seeing the eight-figure number in my bank account, better than when one of my supervisors tried to call me out in a meeting and I got to correct that asshole in front of everyone. Does she regret it? Is she trying to communicate subtly that she made a mistake?

The sun is rising as we make our way to Mrs. Locke's house. Willow knocks on the door.

"I don't think she's awake yet—"

"Willow, what a surprise!" Mrs. Locke beams. "And Hughes! Did you come to bring more Christmas goodies?"

"Actually," Willow says, "we were looking for Maris."

"Oh! She's not been here tonight. I'm hoping that she was out with a boy. Her last marriage ended in divorce, poor thing. And no babies. I'm sure there's a nice man in Harrogate for her." The elderly woman beams at us. "I was hoping to gently nudge her in your direction, Hughes, but I see Beryl has beaten me to the punch. Invite me to the wedding, you two!" She pats my chest. "Maris should be back later. She texted and said she was going to try and bag a turkey for my snow garden party. She's by the old Harrogate Estate, the one the Svenssons took over. Now there's where she needs to find her future husband! I think they all come in for Christmas. A billionaire grandson-in-law. I could have a boat!"

"Willow," I say as we drive silently out to where the industry titans of old built massive country estates with hundreds of acres of forested land. "Do you want to talk about—"

"Mrs. Locke's name is on the list," Willow interjects.

"What?"

"The list I got from the jeweler of who had earrings like these made." She pulls it out of her pocket.

"The earring you found in your stall?" I blow out a breath. "Damn. Did we solve it?"

"I think we did." Willow is grim.

"Shouldn't we call the police?" I slow the car as I approach the trailhead.

"Maris knows how to hunt. She's been gone for a while. She has the motive to kill Dr. Merriweather and Taylor Grace. She's been on the lam since yesterday," Willow reminds me. "She could be halfway to Australia by now. If we call the police and, for some reason, she hasn't bolted yet, they're just going to fumble it and spook her."

She turns to me. "Do you have your recording device ready?"

I nod.

"We're just going to try and get some clues, maybe a confession that we can present with more evidence. We'll make her think we're asking about someone else killing Taylor Grace. Make her think she's home free." Willow outlines the plan.

We step out of the car. The trees rise high into the cold winter morning. It's going to be a tall order to find anyone out here.

"Think it will work?" I stare up at the ancient forest.

"We have to try."

"Or we could go back home, and I can make a winter wonderland up your—"

"Shh!"

Our footfalls are muffled in the early-morning snow. I love walking in the woods in winter, when it's peaceful and beautiful, but today? It feels sinister, like we're being watched.

Suddenly, there's a loud crack of a gun firing. Beside me, Willow lets out a cry, jerks, and falls face-first to the ground.

# CHAPTER 25

# Willow

"Willow! Shit, someone's shooting at us!" Hughes is frantic.

"Really!" I cry. "That's what that was?" I roll over. "I thought it was my ankle when I tripped over that branch." I reach for it. It doesn't feel broken.

"Holy hell." Hughes scoops me up into his arms and cradles me against his chest. "Don't ever scare me like that. I can't lose you."

"Because I'm your partner in crime-solving?" I joke.

He kisses me softly. "Yeah, something like that."

Snow and ice-laden branches creak. Someone is coming.

Hughes crouches over me, sheltering me with his broad chest and shoulders as the dark figure approaches us.

"Maris!" I gasp when the elegant, svelte woman appears out of the trees.

She frowns at us. "You two need to be careful out here. You could have been hurt. There are hunters out, and not everyone is as good of a shot as I am. Next time, wear high-vis clothing."

"Guess I should have worn the red coat," Hughes jokes painfully.

Maris does not smile.

"Okay, she's definitely the murderer," I say, teeth chattering when we climb back into Hughes's cold car.

He cranks up the heat.

"I didn't ask her my questions."

"She knows we know. She knows, and she had a big gun. We need to count ourselves lucky we got out of there." Hughes takes my hands in his and rubs them.

"We don't have evidence for the cops. We have to go back."

"We'll just take them what we have." Hughes pulls out onto the road.

"She'll get away." I look out the rear window, wondering if I'll see her there.

"If we go to the cops and tell them about everything very loudly in the lobby, then the whole town will know by dinnertime that you didn't kill Taylor Grace or Dr. Merriweather, and isn't that what's really important?"

"I mean, I guess."

"Maris did you a good turn getting rid of Taylor Grace. If she runs, she runs." Hughes shrugs.

"She murdered two people. And I'm not completely convinced that Lenore didn't have something to do with it.

We need to review the timeline," I say as Hughes parks on the street.

"Well, also, we only have the cottage for another few hours. Nana has tourists coming in at lunch," he tells me as we walk down the path to the backyard.

"Can we move this operation to the storage room at the Jingle Bites?" I ask, taking off my coat and heading to the murder wall.

"I wasn't really thinking about the murder investigation," Hughes tells me, tugging my sweater over my head.

I shriek. His hands are cold against my bare skin.

"You want to warm me up?"

I turn around in his arms, pull off his shirt, and run my hands over his muscular chest. "I thought," I gasp, grabbing his hair as he kisses my breasts, "that you wanted to—"

"Come down your chimney?"

I yelp as he slides his hand into my panties. "Yeah."

"Well..." My panties and tights come down. My skirt comes up.

"The thing is that we'll have to launder the sheets." A condom packet rips. "And I don't know about you, but I don't really have time to do laundry and solve a murder."

I groan as that huge length slides into me. My back arches as I take all of him. All I can do is whimper as he moves inside of me, kissing my neck, nipping my jaw, squeezing my tits as he takes me over and over, thrusting into me more forcefully until it echoes like a shot every time he slams into me.

I hope this carriage house has been upgraded with insulation because I can't stop the throaty moans as he moves in me until I'm gasping and begging to come, then I'm shuddering around him.

He curses, his hand tightening on my breast, fingers almost painful on my nipple, then he's thrusting into me, erratic, as I milk his cock.

"Damn, Willow."

"Merry Christmas."

He pulls me back by the hair, twisting my head so he can kiss me forcefully. "I'd marry you just so I can fill you up like one of those Santa Claus doughnuts you sell."

"Marriage?"

"Yeah." He gives me a crooked grin.

"Sounds like someone's been watching too many Hallmark movies," I joke, because I don't want to be the person to make this more than what it is—just a fun hookup.

"Mm-hm."

His eyes slide over me as I adjust my clothes.

He's got that glazed look. "I mean, if I got married, why not to my partner in PI?"

"Well, I don't know how many more murders we'll be solving together."

"Come here." He sits back on the couch, legs splayed. He hasn't zipped up. "We still have another hour on the clock."

"You gonna mess me up?" I straddle him.

"Say you'll marry me, and I'll fill you up with my—"

The front door is blown off the hinges. I scream.

Hughes stands up, cursing as he fastens his pants.

"Police!" The Harrogate PD blasts into the living room of the tiny carriage house, guns drawn. "Hands up!"

"Are you serious? You're arresting me again?" I shriek.

"Oh, uh, I don't think so?" Winston lowers his gun, confused.

The police chief sighs. "Hughes, you're under arrest for the murder of Taylor Grace Glass."

# CHAPTER 26
# Hughes

I pace around the cell, rubbing my wrists where the handcuffs were, while out in the police precinct, Nana, Willow, and Beryl argue with the police chief.

"It was his gun that killed Taylor Grace."

"How can they know? How can they possibly know?" Willow cries. "The coroner has people dressed up as Wednesday Addams sleeping in the morgue."

"He pulled the bullet out and compared it to Hughes's gun." The chief is firm.

"That's nonsense!" Nana rails. "Hughes, you have your gun on you at all times."

"I didn't have it when I wasn't wearing my trench coat," I admit, "since that sort of covers it."

"You see," Nana says firmly, "someone stole his gun and is trying to frame him."

"The real murderer is who stole it," Willow says hotly.

"We also have video of him dumping Taylor Grace's cell phone in the Christmas market." The chief sighs, rubs his forehead, and winces when he touches his sunburn.

"I'm sure there's a reasonable explanation." Nana sniffs.

I curse inwardly. I wish I'd spent a little less time having sex and more time reviewing the files I'd copied.

"Check Taylor Grace's phone messages," I tell them.

"We can't break into her phone," the chief admits. "We're trying to get a warrant so we can have a computer firm do it."

For a second, I debate sharing that I have the data then decide against it.

"So, it sounds like all you have is circumstantial evidence," Beryl hollers.

"No, I have evidence evidence." The chief is about to lose it.

"What if we offer you a blow job in exchange for his release?" Nana starts unbuttoning her top.

"Absolutely not." The chief sounds disgusted. "You used to babysit me, Ms. Mary Lou."

"How about Willow?" Berly shoves her forward. "They had sex, and she might be pregnant."

"You're pregnant?" several people in the lobby scream and rush toward Willow.

"I, uh, don't think so?"

"But they're working on it," Nana tells him. "I need to be a great-grandmother. You have to let him out of jail. I don't want my great-grandbaby to be made from sperm produced in a jail cell—"

"Not to mention—" the chief says over them.

"I'm not giving you any more of my special chocolate muffins!" Beryl yells at him.

"—that Hughes is strong enough to have strangled and strung up Dr. Merriweather."

"It wasn't him!" Willow shrieks. "Hughes is not the murderer, but I know who did it! It was Maris."

"Maris?" The police are confused.

"Yes," she says firmly.

"Well, there, you see? You have the wrong person," Nana says firmly. "Let my grandson out of there."

"I have evidence, and I'll give it to you if you let my boyfriend go!" Willow states.

"He stays, and I don't need any muffins," the chief warns.

Nana glares at him.

"I'm trying to watch my sugar." The chief rubs his belly.

"At least release me on bail," I ask.

"That'll be up to the judge. And she's out until Thursday."

"We need to release him. We have the wrong person." Bobby rushes into the room.

"What?"

"We just got back the autopsy from the county. Dr. Jonah Merriweather wasn't electrocuted."

"Suck it, fire department!" The officers whoop.

"Or hung."

"Oh, that's what I thought." Winston looks sad.

"He was poisoned. And everyone knows it's women who do poisoning," Bobby thunders.

"They tested Taylor Grace, too, for the same poison and found it. So Hughes's gun didn't kill anyone."

The chief glares then sighs. "I guess you're free to go."

# CHAPTER 27

# *Willow*

"Poison! They were both poisoned." I pace around the Jingle Bites Café.

Because he stinks of betrayal and jail, Hughes has been dragged to the RV that belongs to the man his grandmother is sleeping with so he can take a sponge bath. I'm stress-baking cookies.

Poison. Poison. Taylor Grace was poisoned.

The leaves in the kitchen. I can't help but think of them... and Josie's bracelet.

"Oh my gosh!" Josie rushes breathlessly into the café. "I just heard. Poison! And everyone says Maris is the culprit."

"I shouldn't have just blamed her like that in public. I don't have watertight evidence." I fill Josie in while my friend stuffs her face with cookies.

The traitorous part of me whispers, *You need to knowwwww.*

Josie dunks a cookie into her latte.

"Do you actually think Maris is the murderer, though?"

"Well, someone's coat had blood on it, not to mention it was difficult to see who was coming and going at the party."

"But I thought Taylor Grace was poisoned. So if Maris poisoned her, why the blood?" Josie asks.

"Someone tried to frame Hughes. Maris is the most likely suspect, but," I dive in, "you came a little late. You didn't happen to see her out at all, did you? Where were you anyway?" I try to ask as casually as possible.

Josie, my oldest and dearest friend, narrows her eyes at me.

I'm sweating.

"Oh my god." Josie's mouth drops open. "You think I poisoned Taylor Grace?"

"No!"

"Yes, you do!" she shrieks. "I'm not organized enough to orchestrate a double homicide poisoning. A shooting, sure, I could handle that. Also, I told you, I was buying a new sweater. I have a receipt here somewhere. See?" She thumbs through her phone. It has a cracked screen, though I know Mace just got her a new one. "Ta-da!"

I breathe out a sigh of relief.

"I don't know why I thought—" I rub my eyes. "I'm sorry. I haven't had any sleep, thanks to Hughes, and then I found your bracelet." I pull it out.

"Oh shit. I had no idea I lost that. Whoops! It must have gotten caught on my sweater or something. So crazy. But also, can we talk about the fact that you had sex with Hughes, please? How was it? How big is he? Scale of zucchini to eggplant?" She mimes with her hands. "Did you take any pictures?"

"You're a married mother."

"I like to know these things, you know. Keep my thumb on the pulse of the market." She snort-laughs into her coffee.

"No photos."

"Next time, then."

"I don't know. Do you think he actually likes me?" I chew on my lip.

"Did he go down on you?"

"Yeah."

"Then he likes you," Josie says firmly. "I bet he's thinking about banging you right now."

"He's probably thinking about how he got roped into my friend drama, and now he's being accused of murder. He's probably getting ready to leave town," I fret.

"Nah, he's going to stick around at least another week." Josie giggles. "Power of the pussy. More than enough time to solve this murder. Get your shit. Let's go bust this case wide open. Also, bring some cookies. Everyone likes your chocolate chunky Santa cookies."

"I don't think she's going to be here," I tell Josie as she marches up the steps to Mrs. Locke's house. "Like, everyone in town is talking about it. Maris must have flown the coop, right?"

"Maybe her granny will know where she went."

But Mrs. Locke doesn't open the door. Instead, it's Maris. Josie and I scream when we see her standing there with a gun.

"Come in," Maris says after a moment.

"Uhhhhhh."

"I'm not going to shoot you in the house. My grandmother would kill me. Tea?" she offers, gesturing to the dining room table, where an array of hunting rifles are on display.

Josie and I look at each other. I know we're both thinking of the poison.

"No, thank you?" I swallow.

"So, uh—" Josie begins.

"So you're here to accuse me of double homicide." Maris raises an eyebrow.

The oil rag rubbing against the metal barrel of the rifle sounds sinister.

"Er, well, maybe I misspoke a little bit." I tap my index fingers together nervously. "I have a lot going on in my life, what with my business partner dying."

Maris snorts. "Business partner, right. I know how that goes. Taylor Grace made your life miserable, didn't she?" she asks accusingly. "You have the most to gain from her death."

"The shop is not profitable. I gain nothing."

"Except peace of mind." Josie claps her hands over her mouth.

"Yeah, no shit. Taylor Grace has no object permanence. She's a big black pit. I know how it was with her." Maris sets the gun down. "You know when it all clicked for me that she was insane and that she was going to drag me down, use me up until I was a shell of myself? One day, she demanded that I get her a personal business credit card, that she felt like I was hiding things from her and I was being controlling and secretive with the money, and she didn't like having to ask me to buy things for the business. So I got her a card, and she turned around and racked up fifty K of credit card debt on bullshit, buying stuff for the business, but really it was for herself. We would have these five-hour-long circular discussions that turned into arguments lasting long into the night, where she'd just say the same thing over and over, just angrier, and act like I was the one ruining her life. Then she had the gall to drag me in front of a therapist that it turns out she's having an affair with?"

"That's exactly what she did to me." I have my head in my hands. "I really wish I'd talked to you before getting involved with her."

"You wouldn't have believed me. You would have thought I was crazy. And I was. Because Taylor Grace made me crazy." Maris taps the table emphatically. "I know that you're not happy about the shop. Fuck the shop. You're relieved you don't ever have to deal with her and her insanity ever again. Sorry." She lets out a breath.

"Sounds like you need a therapist," Josie quips.

"Fuck Jonah Merriweather," Maris scowls. "I'm never going to another therapist. He just enabled her behavior. It sounds like she was worse with you than me." She takes a deep breath. "Look, I admit, I was sneaking into your shop. Can I have my earring back, please?" She holds out a hand. "I wasn't trying to frame you. I wanted to help you prove that she had no rights to anything. I was looking for your files, proof that Taylor Grace was screwing you over like she did me. I didn't want to see you blacklisted like I was around town. I was in there days before Dr. Merriweather's murder. You can have the Christmas cops check the security feeds if you don't believe me."

I purse my lips.

"Trust me. I wanted to see Taylor Grace tried in the court of public opinion, not turned into a martyr," she assured me.

"You had a bloody coat at the holiday party. Hughes saw bloodstains on your sweater."

"Yeah, I didn't realize till I got home that my coat had blood on it from hunting earlier. Melting snow must have bled it out of the fabric onto my sweater. I'll go get it," she offers, standing up. "I haven't gotten around to cleaning it yet. You can't wash it because it's yarn."

We hear her go to the laundry and rustle around.

"I think I believe her," Josie mouths to me. "I don't think she murdered anyone."

Maris comes back out with the sweater. "Go on and test it. It's turkey blood. Take it to the cops and have them test it."

Josie sticks it in a bag.

"But the gun, the shooting!" I protest.

"I like real guns, not toys like your boyfriend carries," Maris sneers. "Anyway. I don't suppose the Jingle Bites Café needs any turkey, does it? I have several dead ones in the smoke shack."

"Minced turkey-meat pastries?" Josie rubs her belly. "Yum!"

"Sure, come by the shop. We'll talk," I tell her.

"And," Josie adds, "if you need a part-time job, I think Willow might be hiring! She just got a boyfriend and won't have as much time to spend at the Jingle Bites Café."

"Oh, so you're fucking the brute." Maris smirks at my expression. "It's a big, bright, beautiful world out there without Taylor Grace," she says as she walks us to the door. "Don't feel guilty. She got what was coming to her."

"Dammit, that's another dead end, then." I sigh when Maris closes the door after us. "Well, let's go back to the Christmas market. I need to relieve Rose."

"You can give me all the dirty deets of kissing Santa Hughes under the Christmas tree." Josie giggles.

"Ugh, there was a dildo."

"Girl! I can't believe I'm just now hearing all this. I'm sorry I was a little MIA earlier, though it did let Hughes get into your Christmas stockings." She links arms with me. "I got wrapped up in Lydia drama."

"Oh yeah?" I can't keep the suspicion out of my voice.

Josie misinterprets it. "I swear I'm not trying to cut you out or anything bad! Lydia just had so much tea to spill about Taylor Grace. I thought maybe I could learn something, since I was, like, a neutral third party, you know?"

"No, no, I'm not mad. I just—I heard Lydia and her husband talking at the Christmas market the night I was locked in the shed," I whisper. "And I just remembered when you said that."

Josie's eyes widen when I recount the conversation. "Yeah, that is suspicious. I know Travis can't—or couldn't—stand Taylor Grace and Lydia was tired of her nonsense, but I never thought they'd murder her."

"We should go see Hughes first."

"Now who's trying to bring men between our friendship?" Josie jokes as we head to the Christmas market. "Or are you trying to get out of the play-by play?"

"I'm not trying to. We will go get all the drinks, but Hughes copied Taylor Grace's phone, and he has her text messages."

Josie is speechless for a second. "Damn. Girl, I hope you gave that man a blow job."

# CHAPTER 28

# Hughes

"I need a house."

"Buy one that you can parcel out and rent to multiple families," Nana tells me, sitting beside me at the table in the Jingle Bites Café. "Like a quadplex. Then you don't have to move out during Christmas. Or get one with an attic that's not up to code."

Willow's not at the cafe. Unfortunately. The entire rest of the town, however, is. I had to agree to take photos with tourists so I could get a table. One lady is recording her true crime podcast on the murders from the seat by the window. The teenager manning the counter looks flustered by the crowd.

"Oh my god, there you are!" Rose cries out when she sees Willow.

Willow and Josie help clear out some of the tourist crowd, then they both come over to me.

"Can't chat long, but we want to give you an update." Willow gives me a quick kiss.

"Wait," I say when they're done. "So, Maris isn't the killer?"

"I don't think so."

"But," Josie says, "we have another lead. Lydia."

"The sister? Hmm." I frown.

"Did you go through the text messages yet?" Willow asks.

"Been reading through the ones between Taylor and the therapist. They were definitely having an affair. Also, for what it's worth, she appeared to be texting Damien right before she was in the shop the night she died. I got the police video—she goes into the shop at 8:17 p.m., but then," I add, "the video cuts out."

"But why?"

"Well, nothing that she texted Damien gives me any clues. It's just insanity." I show her.

"See if there's anything from Lydia."

They watch me type "*L*" into the search bar. Then the messages from Lenore pop up.

"Oooh, wait, what's that?" Willow points.

**Lenore:** *You're having an affair with my husband! Skank!*

**Taylor Grace:** *You're so delusional. It's the menopause. He loves me not you.*

**Taylor Grace:** *He never loved you.*

**Lenore:** *You're delusional if you think he's going to stay with you.*

**Lenore:** *Jonah wants to leave you. He told me so himself.*

Then a few days later:

**Taylor Grace:** *You killed him! I know you killed him!*
**Lenore:** *No, you killed him.*
**Taylor Grace:** *I have proof!*

"Damn." I sit back.

"Lenore needs to be top of the suspect list," Willow says quietly.

"What about Lydia?" Josie asks.

"Hmm." I type in Lydia's name.

The messages between her and Taylor Grace are eerily simliar to the ones between her and me—lots of long-winded lectures passive-aggressively telling her she's a bad mother, that Taylor Grace doesn't agree with the minutiae of how Lydia handled some particular incident that most people would just brush off as kids being kids but triggered Taylor Grace into writing a dissertation of criticism.

"Damn. My sister or not, I'd block her."

"Yeah." Josie grimaces. "Lydia told me that she was thinking of cutting Taylor Grace off."

"Like *off* off?" I mime slitting my throat.

"I don't know about that, but she said that Taylor Grace made her drag herself and her whole family into a therapy session. Her husband was pretty pissed about it because, you know, he's got a stressful job, and Taylor Grace would invite herself over to their house then, like, not leave for hours, just hold Lydia hostage," Josie whispers.

"Look at this." I frown. "There's a phone call from Lydia fifteen minutes before Taylor Grace went to your shop."

"Okay, we have two suspects to investigate. Not for long, though, because the Christmas Bake-Off is tonight, and I cannot just dump all that on poor Hollis. I'd be no better than Taylor Grace." Willow takes out a notepad. "First thing is those herbs. And I know just the witch to ask."

The bell over the door jingles as Hollis comes in with a guinea pig in a basket, munching on lettuce leaves.

"Oh, my little baby!" Willow coos. "Thank you, Hollis, for babysitting. I'm having housing issues right now."

"My pleasure. He's such a cutie." Hollis looks between Hughes and me. "And I see that you two are next in the pipeline for getting married. Willow, you didn't even catch the bouquet at Sandra's wedding last month." She laughs. "That was quick, but I guess when you know, you know!"

"I'll take him from you." Willow picks up the guinea pig. "He can't stay here. Gran thinks the police chief is sleeping with the health inspector, or at least that's what she's spreading around town in retaliation for the arrest of my poor boyfriend here, and we really can't afford to get shut down."

"Yeah, not after our prayers were answered, and we got rid of Taylor Grace," Rose says with a snicker from the counter.

"Did you say *boyfriend*?" Josie squeals then covers her mouth before clapping her hands. "Hollis and I have to be your bridesmaids, Willow!"

"Well, you'd be matron of honor, and I'd be maid of honor, if you want, of course," Hollis corrects. "I love weddings!"

"Oh, also," Willow tells her, "Maris wants to bring by some smoked turkey. Maybe we could branch into pastries? What do you think?"

"Oh, you and Maris are friends? I thought she was the murderer," Hollis says, wide-eyed.

"Well, it seems like that's not quite it." Willow grimaces.

"I'm actually wondering if I should ask her if she wants to work here a little bit?" Willow jokes. "You know, lighten your load. Bond over our collective trauma?"

"Oh, I'm fine, don't you worry about me. I've got it all under control," Hollis trills. "You just go solve that case! I'm going to work on bakery treats for the baking competition tonight."

"Oh my god, thank you for remembering!" Willow hugs her. "You are a lifesaver."

"Don't worry. They're your recipe. We'll enter them under your name and the Jingle Bites Café." Hollis smiles.

"We really should just enter them under yours," Willow tells her. "I don't want to take credit from you. You've been keeping this place afloat."

"Oh!" Hollis beams. "Well. I mean, that's so nice of you, but maybe next year?"

The Christmas market is bustling, even though it's a weekday. People are pouring into town for the Bake-Off and the accompanying free treats.

People are even crowded in the part of the market near Lilith's stall. We wait for the crowd of teenage girls dressed like goth Christmas witches to clear out. And there's Lilith, menacing like a spider in her lair, smoke from the beeswax candles curling around her.

She strokes the back of her black cat, Salem, then turns her dark gaze on us.

"So, you've finally solved the murder."

# CHAPTER 29

## Willow

"Wait, we solved it? Yay!" Josie claps. "Celebratory spider cookies for everyone!"

"It's Lenore. Lenore poisoned Jonah and Taylor Grace," I muse.

Lilith peers at me. "Excuse me, Lenore?"

"Yeah, we saw her brewing a witch's potion," Hughes explains.

"Lenore is not a witch," Lilith sneers.

"Yeah, but she has access to poison through you. She's a good enough witch to kill someone."

"No," Lilith states. "She isn't. She's barely able to keep up in potions class. She can't tell mint from tarragon, and she ordered eye of newt on Amazon. They sent her plastic shrimp, and she couldn't tell the difference. She is not the murderer."

"We have text messages. She and Taylor Grace were fighting, and she had all these poisonous leaves." Hughes waves his phone.

Lilith picks up a twig, which might be her magic wand, with feathers through the leaves. "These are what you found at the murder scene?" Using two black fingernails, Lilith plucks a leaf.

"Yes."

"Then you're the murderer."

Josie and Hughes gasp.

"No, I didn't kill her!" I cry.

"You bought these," she tells me.

"Wait, I what?"

"These are the leaves from the blend to brew mulled wine," Lilith declares.

"Oh! For the Christmas party."

"So how did they end up in the shop?" Hughes asks.

"Don't look at me." Josie shrugs.

"I don't have the answer," Lilith sniffs.

"But you said that we'd solved the murder, so you must know something," I argue.

"No," Lilith says, "but the cards said you will solve the murder today. So I assumed you had."

"Do they say who did it?"

"The cards are not that specific. You will have five children, however—they did tell me that much."

"Wow." I feel lightheaded.

"Also, Josie, the next time you misplace your baby, you'll find him in a strawberry patch."

"What about me? Do I get a fortune?" Hughes jokes.

"Yes, you're going to die relatively soon."

Hughes looks at me askance.

Lord Mycroft lets out a cry of "Eep."

"No, Salem, do not eat the overweight guinea pig."

The black cat hisses.

"Oh, did you already eat all your lettuce?" I coo at Mycroft.

Lilith gives him a handful of seeds. The guinea pig snarfs them down.

Salem looks much too interested in my pet.

"Damn, Lilith," Hughes says, sounding tense. "My last day on earth, huh?"

"Don't listen to Lilith," I tell Hughes. "Sometimes, she just says crazy things. It's all that incense—it's not good for you." I take his hand. "Besides, she said I'm having five kids, so that means you're going to stick around."

"Unless you donated sperm that we don't know about," Lilith adds.

"I mean, it is cold, so you could dig the condom out of the dumpster," Josie jokes. "Probably still good."

Hughes picks up the guinea pig and snuggles him to his chest. He scratches Mycroft's ears as we head through the market.

"Lydia and Travis are at the ice-skating rink," Josie tells me.

I take a breath of the cold spice-and-juniper-filled air. "Let's go see if we can get a confession out of her."

"We're close. I can feel it. I could also be hungry. Right, Lord M?" I scratch the guinea pig's cheek.

Lydia is leaning against the barrier to the ice rink, whispering to her husband.

"Hey!" Josie puts on her extra-happy face. "Lydia! Oh, the kids look so cute in their little skating outfits!"

I hug Lydia and wave to Travis.

"Oh my gosh," Josie says, "so Willow and I went to talk to Maris today."

"Ugh, I tried to go talk to her before Taylor Grace—"

"Went to hell," Travis mutters.

"Oh, Travis." But Lydia doesn't seem super angry. "Anyway, how is she?" she grimaces. "Taylor Grace really screwed her over."

"Well, it turns out she didn't murder Taylor Grace."

"Yeah, we pulled Taylor Grace's phone records," I tell her, "because we were hoping to find something to uncover the murderer."

Lydia blanches.

Travis's eyes bug out. "The police have her phone records?" He sounds upset. "They haven't cracked her phone. They asked us for the password, and they said they couldn't crack it without that."

"Well, we have a computer wiz." I point at Hughes.

"So I guess you saw—" Lydia sags.

"The call? Yes."

"I didn't kill my sister, I swear. I mean, yeah, it's not a secret that we're happy she's not here anymore. I mean, she was nuts."

"Josie told me."

"She wanted our kids to be her emotional support animals. I think she was gearing up to take them from us," Travis says stubbornly.

"I don't know about that. Taylor Grace doesn't actually like kids." Lydia tugs at her hair.

"She likes drama."

"I called her because I wanted to talk to her. She was going nuts, complaining that Josie, Hollis, and Maris were all trying to take her away from me," Lydia explains. "It began because Hollis and I started hanging out."

"And Taylor Grace is the one who initiated it," Travis interjects.

"Yeah, but Hollis loves kids! She's such a wonderful friend. Taylor Grace got jealous. Said Hollis wanted to steal me from her. You should have heard her when she and that therapist ganged up on me." Lydia sags against the skating rink wall. "Then Maris came back to town, and Taylor Grace found out that I was trying to get in contact with her, and she just flipped out, accused me of being a traitor. Same thing with Josie—said she and Willow were trying to steal me and the kids from her."

"Did she say anything when you went to talk to her?" Josie takes her hand.

"Taylor Grace wanted to meet in the shop, and when I got there, she was dead," Lydia admits. "I just walked away, went to the party."

"Who knew you were going to meet her at the shop?" I ask.

"Well, Travis did..." Lydia looks at him.

"I didn't kill her. I was at the Christmas market, nearby, waiting for the meeting to be done." Travis crosses his arms.

"No one thinks you killed her." Lydia pats his leg. "The thing is, though," she says slowly, "she wasn't shot when I got there. She was face down on the floor, dead, but no gunshot wounds."

"And you didn't see anyone else when you were coming or leaving?"

"No." Lydia shakes her head. She looks teary-eyed. "I guess you're going to go to the police?"

"Can't. There's no evidence." I shrug.

"But I'm on the video."

"No, the video cut out." Hughes frowns.

"Oh, thank God. I mean—" Her eyes shift. "Oh no, now we don't know who killed my sister."

"See, Lydia, I told you, you were worried for no reason. The murderer obviously would have thought of the cameras," Travis says. "That's why Jonah was hung in the tree. The branches would obscure the cameras."

"This is the same MO."

"Ugh, what are we going to do?" We walk back through the market. "We are completely at a dead end."

"Enjoy the Christmas market, eat cookies, regroup tomorrow. You two can get started on the five babies." Josie skips beside me.

"I need to go help Hollis." I take back Lord Mycroft.

"She's the MVP. You need to get her a really nice Christmas present."

"Half of me wants to just give her the shop," I confess. "She's basically earned it."

"What will you do instead?" Hughes asks.

"Maybe just work there part-time."

"Have babies." Josie pokes me.

"Hughes! Hughes!" someone calls.

Then Mary Lou is rushing up, flustered. "Oh my god, something horrible has happened!" she cries. "You have to come with me at once."

# CHAPTER 30

## Willow

"What's wrong?" Hughes asks anxiously as his grandmother rushes over. "Nana, what happened?"

"Oh, it's horrible! You have to come help. Jordan brought his pet alpaca—I mean, honestly, he dresses the thing up like a reindeer, like people aren't going to notice it's a completely different animal—and it's knocked over the judges' station and is eating the mints. We need all hands on deck! Now it's time to show everyone those muscles aren't just for vanity's sake," she says as she drags him off.

He gives me a quick kiss before he goes.

"You can boink him tonight." Josie waggles her eyebrows as I look after him longingly.

I know my face is Rudolph red.

"Oops, I promised I would help with kid wrangling so some of my sisters-in-law could enter the baking competition.

I need to run. I'll see you in a few hours?" Josie tells me, checking her phone.

"Yeah, hopefully Hollis isn't freaking out too much."

"She always has everything under control," Josie waves.

I call Hollis just to make sure she's at the shop and not in the market so I don't have to walk back and forth.

It goes to voicemail.

**Hollis:** *Sorry! There is an apple cider emergency!*

**Willow:** *Uh-oh, I bet it has something to do with that alpaca.*

**Hollis:** **angry emoji**

**Hollis:** *Do you think you could run to Amy's farm and get some more herbs? They are all out at the general store. There is going to be a fight!*

**Hollis:** *I need it to finish off the Holly Jolly Cupcakes.*

**Willow:** *On my way!*

It's snowing heavily as I drive Gran's old Cadillac down the winding country roads to Amy's farm.

The greenhouses there grow flowers and other natural decorations that Amy uses for her big showstopping Manhattan weddings.

"I don't know if I want a big wedding like that," I tell the guinea pig.

He snuffles, looking for food in his basket.

"But it's not like we're going to elope or something. I mean, half the town will want to come. Just Josie and her family are going to fill up the church. Better have it outside.

Gosh, I'm so silly, sitting here, planning a wedding when there's a murderer or two running loose. I don't even know what I'm entering into the Bake-Off competition, and I don't have a ring or anything."

I pull into a parking space and duck out into the falling snow.

"Oh! Hey!" Amy waves when I enter one of the warm greenhouses.

"Did Hollis mention I was coming?" I greet her.

"No," she says, confused. "I'm glad you caught me. I was about to head out to the Bake-Off."

"It's crazy down there. Also, there's not a leaf of mint anywhere in town."

"Oh," she says. "Weird. Well, what kind of mint do you want? We have spearmint, chocolate mint, pineapple mint, banana mint—Hollis was just up here earlier. It's too bad she didn't realize that y'all were out. It would have saved you a trip."

"I think just regular mint?" I shrug.

"Boo! I have lemon mint and water mint and—oh, Mycroft, you need to stay away from my pumpkins!"

The guinea pig is half hanging out of his basket, little rodent mouth open to snag a bite of a pretty white-and-yellow-swirled pumpkin.

"That looks like Cinderella's carriage." I admire it.

"He's a hybrid." Amy pats the pumpkin affectionately.

"You must be a Halloween girlie," I remark. "It's not even Christmas, and the pumpkins are out."

"Getting started on next year's batch. So don't ruin my hard work." Amy snuggles the guinea pig.

"Oh, do you two know each other?"

"Hollis brings him by sometimes when she's babysitting." She snips off a few leaves and feeds them to the guinea pig, who scarfs them down.

"If you have any reject pumpkins," I tell her, "I've been wanting to make pumpkin tarts at the shop. Taylor Grace thought it was a stupid idea, but apparently, I don't have to listen to her anymore."

"No!" Amy barks at me. "Absolutely not."

"Oh, okay, sorry." I take a step back.

Amy softens. "Sorry to scare you, but never eat squash that's not from seeds. You can get cucurbit poison—toxic squash syndrome. Only eat squash you grow from a seed that you buy," she says urgently.

"Well, I'm not a gardener, so I don't think that will be a problem," I joke.

"Guinea pigs can have them, though," Amy coos and feeds Mycroft some more leaves. "I'll give you a bag of clippings for him. And here's some mint. I personally think that the apple mint will go amazing with your desserts. Good luck! I can't wait to taste everything!"

I hum along to the Christmas carols on the radio while Lord Mycroft sits happily in his bed of lettuce leaves and munches.

"Not lettuce leaves," I correct myself.

I turn the radio tuner to another Christmas station. Yeah, Gran's old-school, no touch screens in this car. Or airbags, either, so I need to be careful.

In the side-view mirror, I see a huge pickup truck going pretty fast. It speeds past me and clips the side of the Cadillac. I scream as the car jerks. The Cadillac swerves as I try to regain control on the icy road. We fishtail into a snowbank on the side of the road.

"Oh my god, oh my god," I repeat over and over.

The truck doesn't even slow. I watch the taillights speed down the country road.

"Oh my gosh, did someone try to kill us?" I shriek at the guinea pig. "Help!" I call forlornly into the forest. "Oh, no, your salad is all over the floor."

My hands are shaking. I don't know why I'm fixated on the salad. I need to call 911, right? Wait, Gran doesn't have this thing insured. I need to phone a friend. I dial Hollis.

"Hey, where are you?" she asks.

"Just coming back from the farm with the mint." I stare at the leaf in my hand. Then, suddenly, I know who killed Taylor Grace and Dr. Merriweather. "I just wanted to make sure you weren't freaking out." I try to keep the tremor out of my voice. "Snow's pretty heavy."

"Gotcha." There's a long pause on the phone. "Well, better concentrate on driving. Lots of crazy people out here. Hope no one runs you over."

"Frickety frickety St. Nick." I pace around in the cold, trying to call Hughes. No answer.

I need to get back to the Christmas market.

Sitting behind the wheel once more, I say a little prayer to the Christmas gods.

"Okay. Let's do this." I rev the engine of the old Cadillac. "Come on, go!"

The back tires catch, and the massive tank lurches back onto the road.

"Whoo!" I holler as I floor it.

As I race back to town, I try Hughes over and over, but he never picks up the phone.

# CHAPTER 31

## Willow

The Christmas market is mayhem. Bookies run around taking bets on the baking competition. Tourists and townspeople crowd up to the stage next to the large Christmas tree to get a good spot.

"Have you seen Hughes?" I shout to Josie.

She's surrounded by a sea of Mace's younger brothers, all hyped up on sugary festive snacks and hot chocolate.

"No, he wasn't here when I came back," she says, frazzled.

"I have to tell you something," I tell her urgently.

"Give me like ten minutes," she pleads as several kids start wailing. One of the older kids has her baby strapped to his chest, and he starts complaining loudly.

"When you have women falling all over you because you know how to change a diaper, you'll thank me one day. Also, the baby likes you better than me, so Merry Christmas."

"Oh, hi!" Lydia says to me, her own overstimulated kids in tow. "Have you seen Travis?"

"No, have you seen Hughes?"

"Ugh, men! They just wander off!"

I make my way to where all the bakers are being staged.

"Where are your Christmas cookies?" Ida yells into the tinny megaphone. "All baked goods must be on the tables, or you're disqualified!"

"Oh, there you are!" Hollis chirps.

I peer at her as she emerges from the shadows, carrying a tiered tray of cupcakes.

"Good, you have the mint!" She beams at me. "Thank you so much for getting that."

"Bakers, ready your pastries!" Ida blares.

"I'm looking for Hughes," I tell her, trying not to give it away that *I know*.

"Come on! This is the first day of the rest of our lives. Forget Hughes. You only just met him. If he wants to run off with another girl, let him."

"He's with another girl?" I feel sick.

Hollis blinks at me. "I mean, he was with Taylor Grace while he was with you, right? It's the most likely scenario. You can't trust men like that."

Do I have it all wrong? Was it a holiday-fueled hallucination? "I, uh—"

"Don't be sad, Willow. He's not good enough for you anyway. It's just you and me now, making holiday magic together." She pats my arm sympathetically.

"I need to wash the mint," I tell her, hurrying away.

I duck around the back of the stage. Hughes didn't run off. I know he didn't run off. And I know I'm not wrong about Hollis. She's been poisoning people with the toxic pumpkins. And now she's done something to Hughes. I race around, trying to find him, but there's no sign of him.

I'm about to head back to the Bake-Off when I hear the roar of a truck. I duck behind an elf trash can and watch a pickup back up to a pile of pallets covered with a tarp. A man dressed all in black jumps out of the still-running truck then slowly manhandles something out of the pile.

*Hughes.* Crap. I did have it wrong. It wasn't Hollis. It was…

I don't know who that is, but I don't have time to figure it out. The murderer is busy loading an unconscious Hughes into the bed of the pickup truck.

I sneak around, climb into the cab, and floor it.

The tires squeal as the man screams, "You bitch!"

His voice is muffled, but the shots that ring out from the gun he fires aren't. I shriek a curse, ducking as bullets ping off the car's frame.

"Hughes!" I cry. Looking in the rearview mirror, I don't see Hughes's body lying lifelessly on the snow. "He must still be in the bed of the truck," I say, trying to angle the mirror to find him.

*Crash!*

Snow, branches, and Christmas lights rain down on me as I drive headfirst into the Christmas tree. The tree doesn't even budge. The truck crumples like tissue paper, though.

The man runs at me, gun raised.

I rush to rescue Hughes from the back of the truck. Branches snag on me. "I need to lift weights," I groan as I heft Hughes's unconscious body and stagger out. But there's no way I'll be fast enough. I stare as the man in black aims his gun.

*Crack!* goes the sound of the rifle.

The man screams. Blood spurts out of his wrist.

Is there another murderer? I look around wildly.

The man pulls the hood from his face and continues screaming. "You shot me!"

"I didn't shoot you."

"Yes, yes, you did," Travis seethes. He looks crazy. "You shot me. You and Hughes, you orchestrated these murders."

"What the—no, I didn't!"

"That's what I'm telling the town, and they're going to believe me," he snarls, spittle flying from his mouth.

Somewhere above me, in the tree, I hear a woman yell, "Go after him! I'll take care of Hughes."

"What do you mean, take care of him?"

Someone swings down from the high branches.

"Is that you, Maris?"

"Go!" she yells.

Once again, I curse the fact that I am not in good enough shape as I hoof it after Travis while he runs screaming and bleeding back to the Bake-Off.

"The murderer struck again!" Travis is yelling into the microphone in front of the judges when I practically collapse back onto the stage.

"That's not—" I wheeze.

"Willow and Hughes, they orchestrated the murders of Taylor Grace and Dr. Merriweather, and when I confronted them about it, they shot me!"

"He was trying to kidnap Hughes, and Maris shot him. She's a witness!" I try to grab the megaphone.

"Wait, that was Maris who shot me? She kills deer and turkeys. She knows how to shoot. She could have killed me!" Travis whips around to yell at Hollis. "You should have told me she was in on it! I would have Amazon Primed a bulletproof vest."

"I—I—I—" Hollis stammers.

"I knew it! I knew you were poisoning them with the toxic squash!" I holler.

The crowd titters.

Someone from the crowd says drunkenly, "Is this the Christmas pageant?"

"I never—police!" Hollis screeches. "Where are the Christmas police? This man is insane. Check his desk at Svensson PharmaTech. I bet you'll find Dr. Merriweather's phone in his office."

"No, you won't. Unless you planted it there," Travis fumes at Hollis.

"I would never. I'm no murderer. I'm a baker." She presses her hands to her chest.

"I knew you were going to pull this shit. That's why I saved the video I cut from the security feed." Travis advances on her, teeth bared.

"You what?" Hollis squawks. "I told you to delete it or we would both go to jail!"

"Well, I'm not taking the fall for you. I want a plea bargain," he demands as the Christmas cops advance on the stage.

"Hollis, why?" I ask.

Hollis is teary-eyed. "I killed them for you, Willow," she says, "because we're best friends. Dr. Merriweather was talking Taylor Grace into stealing our shop. Then Taylor Grace had to go because she was stressing you out. And Hughes—he isn't good for you. He's monopolizing your time. You're better off without him in your life."

"Why'd you get Travis involved in the murder?" I ask her.

"I blackmailed him into helping because he was having an affair with Taylor Grace." Hollis glares at him.

"You piece of shit!" Lydia hollers from the crowd.

"It wasn't an affair," Travis argues. "It was one time," he tells Lydia. "She came onto me once when I was drunk. Can I get a temporary insanity plea? Taylor Grace literally drove me insane!"

Lydia hurls her cup of apple cider at him.

"Ow!"

The Christmas cops move in, red-and-green handcuffs out.

"I didn't murder anyone!" Travis begs.

"You strung up Dr. Merriweather's body and shot Taylor Grace's corpse," Hollis argues. "You're an accomplice."

"Yeah, but I didn't kill anyone! Lydia, please don't divorce me," he pleads as the Christmas cops snap the handcuffs on him.

"I'm innocent too." Hollis bursts into tears. "It was self-defense. I'm your best friend, Willow."

"No, you're not. I am!" Josie hollers.

"Poisoning Hughes was not self-defense!" I tell her, furious. "Oh! Hughes, poor Hughes! Remy, we need to call the ambulance." I start freaking out.

"What? I thought it was a prank. I didn't know that he was actually dying," Travis complains as the Christmas cops haul him and Hollis away.

"Willow!" someone cries painfully from the back of the stage. "Willow, I'm coming to save you."

Maris is a few steps behind Hughes.

"He insisted." She rolls her eyes.

"Oh, Hughes, you're too late."

"No," he groans.

"Just lie down," I beg.

"Ugh." He slumps onto the ground.

"You've been poisoned. Where are the EMTs?" I look around wildly.

"EMT? Pshaw." Gran appears with a bottle in a paper bag. "Bought the last bottle of moonshine from Lilith. She puts extra special herbs and spices in it." She shakes the bottle.

"It looks like pond water. I don't think we should—"

Gran tips it down Hughes's throat.

He gurgles then shoots straight up. "Oh my god!"

"That'll put the spirit of Christmas in you." She pats his back.

There are complaints from the tourists watching the Bake-Off. "Give us the cookies! We want cookies!"

Hughes pukes on the stage.

The crowd groans.

"Don't worry," Ida says into the microphone. "Cookies are happening as soon as we clean out the riffraff. The Jingle Bites Café is, of course, disqualified on account of the cupcakes probably being poisoned."

"Maybe a little more. Second time's the charm." Gran holds the moonshine to Hughes's mouth.

"Gran, stop giving that to him!" I bat the bottle away.

"See?" Gran drags Hughes upright and pats his cheeks. "He's all right."

"I don't think that's how this works."

"He's not all right," Hughes groans then collapses.

# CHAPTER 32
# Hughes

*The snow is coming down thick, muting the sirens and the city's sins alike. She is gone now—the dame who dragged me into this tinsel-tangled mess—and I'm left with her ghost and a bullet graze that stings like regret. I should've seen it coming, but love and bourbon make a lousy pair of glasses. And love is all I see. My girl Friday, my partner in crime-solving, stands by the window. She patched me up and poured me coffee strong enough to burn the truth out of my throat. Outside, Christmas lights blink like confessions, and for once, I believe in love and Christmas miracles...*

"Men are so dramatic."

Nana fusses as she rearranges the pillows behind my head, sending Lord Mycroft grunting from where he's made a nest next to my hip.

"Ow! I've been in the hospital for days," I tell her incredulously. "I almost died. I got shot."

"No, you didn't," she snorts. "That was a scrape from a tree branch, and anyway, I told Jenine's daughter—she's the head nurse there, you know—I told her I had Airbnb-ers until Tuesday and she needed to keep you there because I didn't have anywhere to put you."

"Thanks, Nana."

She smooches the top of my head.

"There's my big brave PI." Willow climbs onto the bed to wrap her arms around me.

"When you say it that way, it sounds condescending," I say, kissing her mouth. "Thanks for rescuing me."

"I had ulterior motives. Five children, remember?" She curls up in the crook of my arm.

"I was told no strenuous activity," I say, but I kiss her neck.

At that moment, Nana barges back in.

"I made you chicken-and-dumpling soup. Eat up—you need your fortification for the Christmas pageant tonight."

Willow kisses me again.

"So, I hear you're keeping the shop?"

"Well, obviously. I can't give it to Hollis, though maybe she could run it from jail," she muses. "She was a fantastic employee."

"She tried to kill me," I complain.

"Hey, good help is hard to find in this town, especially during the holiday season." She pokes me.

"I really don't want you to work. I want you to stay with me." I nuzzle her nose.

"Fresh bread!" Nana comes back in with a steaming basket. "They're French onion rolls. And did I hear you say you need someone to watch the shop so you can get cracking on those great-grandbabies?"

"Er—"

"Fantastic!" Nana beams. "I already have volunteers lined up. Several seniors in town are itching for a chance to work at the murder café."

"Well, Maris is going to help." Willow grimaces.

"You need more than Maris. We've got several ex-strippers who will hit the Christmas market paths to do promotions."

"Nana…" I turn to Willow. "I can help, too—any excuse to see you."

"Any excuse?" She waggles her eyebrows.

"This isn't exactly what I meant," I tell Willow as she and Josie try to fit me into a hangman's costume that's a size too small.

"Just duct-tape it and keep it moving!" Ida blares from a megaphone. "The Christmas pageant cannot start forty-five minutes late like it did last year!"

Willow giggles. "You look so hot in that costume."

"You see what you started? Now she has a murder fetish."

"No, I have a private-eye fetish. You should wear that trench coat tonight." She giggles. "And the hat."

I lean in to kiss her. "Anything for you. I love you."

"I love you too."

"Merry Christmas."

She salutes me as I head onstage, raise the axe, and take my position.

A small blond-haired, gray-eyed child in angel's wings trots out to the middle of the stage. He takes a deep breath. "*Peppermint and Poison: A Murder in Three Acts.*"

I raise the fake axe and slowly bring it down while the little boy starts reciting his lines, setting the stage for the gruesome Christmas murder.

"Can you believe," the guy who's been press-ganged into playing Jonah whispers to me, "that they only just finished writing it yesterday?"

"Oh, I believe it."

The townspeople cheer as "Jonah" pretends to die while the child angel screams dramatically.

"That's my boyfriend!" Willow whoops. "You're doing amazing!" She gives me two thumbs up.

"Merry Christmas!" I boom out my line. "With a side of murder!"

# EPILOGUE

## *Willow*

"This wedding was a mistake."

Josie nearly spits out her peppermint mimosa. "You don't want to marry him?"

"No, I do," I hiss, yanking at a piece of tulle that's trying to smother me. "I just should've eloped. Maybe to a courthouse. Or a cave. Or the moon."

"Who doesn't love a Christmas wedding?" she asks, twirling in her red-and-white-striped dress. "It's festive! Magical! Wholesome!"

"There are at least a hundred thousand people here," I mutter. "I don't even know all these people. That guy over there just asked if I'm the understudy for Mrs. Claus."

Josie pauses. "Be honest—do I look like a stripper in a candy cane wrapper?"

Before I can answer, the bagpipes start.

A platform has been built in front of the enormous Christmas tree at the center of the square, surrounded by garlands, twinkling lights, and about seven thousand spectators clutching hot cider. The banner reads: A Very Merry Wedding, Hughes & Willow.

I hitch up my dress. The bagpipes blare out something that sounds like a mix of "Jingle Bells" and the "Wedding March." Fake snow falls. Drunken townspeople cheer.

Trying not to trip over the hem of my dress, I slowly make my way up the short ramp to Hughes, my fiancé, my soon-to-be husband, waiting for me with a soft smile.

Mayor Loring, wearing a Santa hat, beams at us as she begins the ceremony.

I blink back tears when we get to the vows and take a breath. "Hughes, when we first met, I thought you were an uptight, judgmental wannabe detective with the emotional range of a snow shovel."

The crowd laughs. He tries not to.

"And you thought I was a murderer, so really, we started off strong."

He laughs now, shoulders shaking.

"But somewhere between arguments in the middle of the Christmas market, I realized you weren't just stubborn—you were good. The kind of good that risks everything to find the truth. So, yes, I promise to love you, to annoy you daily, and to remind you that I was right about the murderer."

"Eh, I think I might have been right about a few things." Then he takes my hands. "Willow," he says, voice soft, "you drove me insane. You talked too much, questioned everything, and got me arrested. I wanted to throttle you. And then, somewhere between chasing suspects and hiding in a bakery freezer, I realized I didn't want to solve anything without you. You make chaos feel like home. You make danger feel worth it. I promise to protect you—even when you don't want me to—and to stand beside you, whether we're solving murders or surviving your gran's booze-laden Christmas punch. You're my favorite mystery, and I never want to stop trying to figure you out."

Mayor Loring grins. "By the power vested in me by the great city of Harrogate, I now pronounce you husband and wife. You may kiss your bride."

Hughes doesn't wait for a second invitation. His hands are at my waist, and the kiss is warm and certain and tastes like cinnamon and second chances. Snow swirls around us, and the whole square cheers.

The market transforms into a glittering party. The band, a group of enthusiastic teenagers—hey, it was them or the polka band of eighty-year-olds—plays "Jingle Bell Rock." Fairy lights shimmer over the cider booth, and Gran stands on a table, yelling, "Drink up, it's what Jesus would've wanted!"

I'm halfway through a soft pretzel when someone screams, "Oh my god—Mary Lou!"

Everyone turns. Hughes's grandmother is face down in the Christmas punch bowl. Hughes rushes to her.

"Murder!" someone shouts. "She's been murdered!"

People gasp.

Mary Lou drags her head up out of the punch bowl. I almost collapse with relief.

"Murder?" She blinks and hiccups. "There's been another murder?"

"She's just drunk!" Gran shouts.

The crowd bursts into laughter. Someone hands her another mug. She clinks it against the bagpiper's and starts a conga line.

Hughes slips an arm around me, his laugh muffled against my hair. "So, this is married life?"

"Apparently," I say. "Till death do us part."

He kisses me again, right there in the snow, while the townspeople dance past, singing along to the music.

"I love you, and I think we already got the death part down."

# Acknowledgements

*A big thank you to Red Adept Editing for editing and proofreading.*

*And finally a big thank you to all the readers! I had a great time writing this hilarious book! Please try not to choke on your wine while reading!!!*

# About the Author

If you like steamy romantic comedy novels with a creative streak, then I'm your girl!

Architect by day, writer by night, I love matcha green tea, chocolate, and books! So many books...

Sign up for my mailing list to get special bonus content, free books, giveaways, and more!

http://alinajacobs.com/mailinglist.html

Printed in Dunstable, United Kingdom

74323593R00137